CLAIMING HIS PRIZE

DANGEROUS GAMES BOOK 3

SINISTRE ANGE

Cover art: Furious Fotog
Editing: Personal Touch Editing

1

The sun slanting across Allison's face woke her much earlier than she was used to and reminded her, she wanted to hang curtains today. Although Todd had hired movers, Allison insisted she wanted just the two of them to set up the house. She wanted the full experience of moving in with him—the discussions, and occasional arguments, about where everything was supposed to go.

Just yesterday, they'd argued over the placement of the couch until he'd bent her over the arm of it and spanked her until she agreed with him about its location. Of course, that had turned them on, so he'd also ended up fucking her as she was draped over the arm of the couch, his hands squeezing her reddened buttocks, igniting that wonderful mix of pleasure and pain she enjoyed so much, until she came screaming as he rutted into her from behind. Then he'd made her finish the rest of their discussions without putting her pants back on as cum dripped down the insides of legs.

Which is why they'd never gotten around to hanging the curtains.

Turning away from the window, Allison came face to face with her boyfriend. Boyfriend was such a tame word for the feelings she had for Todd—love, adoration, occasional extreme frustration, and a deeply intense craving to touch and be touched by him. Sometimes, she thought she'd never get enough of it, and it didn't seem to matter whether he was holding her in his arms or beating her ass, she wanted it.

This wasn't the kind of relationship she'd pictured. Two years ago, she had been willing to live the life her parents chose for her—marrying a man just like her father and living in a big house, throwing big parties and being the perfect little housewife, whose life was dedicated to her husband and furthering themselves in 'society.' In all honesty, it had been like something out of a Victorian romance novel, except she hadn't been truly happy, and it hadn't been at all romantic. She'd hated the constrictions on her life, hated feeling like she was only valued as an asset to the family, hated that other people her age were able to have crazy wild adventures, but she was stuck going to parties and schmoozing clients for her father at his parties.

Then she'd met Todd—a man who had both intrigued and repulsed her. Staring at his face, with its strong features, firm jawline, and brushing of dark stubble, she remembered how she'd initially thought she was too good for him, he was beneath her, but even then, she'd been intrigued. Then she'd drunkenly admitted some of her deepest, darkest fantasies—about losing control and being blackmailed into doing the crazy things she'd always wanted to do—and for some reason, most of them seemed to be sexual. Only later had she realized. Freeing that part of her, allowed her to free herself in other ways, too.

Todd had left her to work overseas, and she had been unable to continue life as it had been before him. Instead, she got a job, moved out of her parents' house and in with her friend. Diana was of the same social set, but her parents were much less pressed over social standing and 'moving up in the world.' Eventually, Allison broken up with the boyfriend her parents had chosen for her. Poor Roger. He'd become a good friend by the end of their time together, but he had never lit her up from the inside the way Todd did. By the time Todd came back home, Allison had been ready for him—ready to try having a real relationship with a man *she'd* chosen—and she could only thank her lucky stars, he had felt the same way.

Unfortunately, telling her parents about her new relationship had caused a scene—more than a scene. Her parents had basically kicked her out of their lives until she 'came to her senses' and did what they wanted—which meant breaking up with Todd. Sometimes, she wondered if they would have stopped paying for her schooling if it hadn't already been paid for her last semester in college. Thankfully, she'd started working the past summer, and now she was working and attending classes. If she had still been under her parents' roof and beholden to their money, defying them would have been a lot more difficult.

Allison didn't regret her decision, although every time she thought about her parents, it still hurt. She'd thought she meant more to them. She wasn't sure if it was her uncharacteristic defiance that had enraged her father, or if he truly cared more for his job and business contacts than he did about her. With both sides holding out for an apology, it didn't seem like there would be peace any time soon. Strangely, the member of her family she was closest to now her was her step-cousin, Chad, whom she'd disliked for most of her life up until the past year. She had Todd to thank for that. Although his methods were perhaps not what she would have chosen, they'd become friends, and she appreciated that now.

These were maudlin thoughts for a morning she wanted to spend with her boyfriend. They had a lot to get done today. They'd both taken a couple days off of work to help with the move-in process, but tomorrow was their last day off. She had been hoping to finish early, so they could spend tomorrow evening relaxing in their new home. Although Todd had paid for the house, he'd made it clear he considered it theirs, and she'd ended up contributing to the furnishings and insisted on paying for the entire first grocery bill— which had been substantial. While Todd was making a lot more money, she wanted to be a financial part of putting their home together. Otherwise, it just felt like everything was his, and she was a guest. Being able to pay for some of it really made it *theirs*.

She reached out and put her hand on his chest, sliding the covers down to bare his skin. Todd was a heavy sleeper. The alarm clock he used was incredibly loud, and she still ended up waking him up more often than not because the alarm woke her first, then she kicked him until he woke up and turned it off. While it might be a little creepy, she liked to watch him sleep. His face was so serene in slumber, and with the sun shining into the room, he looked like a dark angel—or maybe a fallen one—with his dark hair, tanned skin, and handsome features. Just looking at him sent a surge of lust through her. She was going to live with him, waking up to this every morning.

Smiling, she pushed the covers down to his thighs, unsurprised to find he had some serious morning wood. Carefully, she got to her hands and knees, sliding down the bed until her head was hovering above his groin. Glancing up at his prone body, she smiled as she saw he was still asleep. This was going to be fun.

Starting at the very base, she gave his cock one long, slow lick all the way to the tip as it jumped and jerked. Todd made a mumbling sound as she sucked the tip into her mouth, then began to take him into her mouth. She managed three good bobs of her head up and down his long shaft before she felt his body tense beneath her palms. A hand came down on the back of her head, grabbing her hair and wrapping it around his fist several times until he had her on a short leash, her every movement now controlled by him.

The established dominance had an immediate effect on her libido—her nipples hardened, and her pussy creamed even more. Mouth full of cock, she raised her eyes to meet Todd's, enjoying the lust in his expression and the threatening glitter in his eyes.

"Naughty, naughty, trying to get yourself an early morning treat without permission." His hand held her steady, so she couldn't lift her mouth off of him to reply. Instead, she just batted her eyes, and he laughed—she probably looked ridiculous doing that. She giggled, which had the effect of vibrating his cock in her mouth. He groaned as he lifted her head up, then down again, forcing her to take more and more of his meat into her throat. Her own body throbbed for attention, but both of Todd's hands were on her head. Allison

4

whimpered, shuffling on the bed to turn her lower body toward him, wiggling her hips to try to entice him. Todd released one hand from her head and slapped her ass. Allison moaned and wiggled her hips again, asking for more.

"Little slut." He chuckled, which just turned her on even more. From Todd, it always sounded like a compliment, not an insult. He pulled her up by her hair, yanking her toward him with enough brute force, it hurt just enough to feel good before he took her mouth in a punishing kiss. His free hand went unerringly to her breast, pinching her nipple so hard, she yelped and writhed, her open mouth allowing his tongue to plunge in deeply. The sharp pinch on her nipple was like a tight clamp, and her breast ached as his unrelenting grip tugged and pulled the tender bud.

He pushed her, and Allison found herself on her back with Todd hovering over her. He had the best throw down. It always happened so fast, she never knew when it was coming, but it always took her breath away. Gripping her wrists, Todd held them above her head and attached them to the cuffs he had dangling. They'd been installed yesterday, bolted to the wall just above the bed, easily hidden by pillows when company came over and easily accessible at any time Todd felt like chaining her up.

She moaned as he secured her, the helpless vulnerability of her situation causing her pussy to flood even more. Todd stretched out over her, his lower body pinning hers to the bed, and she could feel the velvety head of his cock pressing against her pussy lips, but he didn't thrust forward. Instead, he cupped her breasts and massaged them gently, her one abused nipple feeling more swollen and sensitive than the other.

"Is this what you were hoping for, you bad girl?" His breath was hot on her neck as he kissed and nipped at the sensitive skin there.

"Close enough," Allison said, panting. "Fuck me... please, Todd, fuck me." She lifted her hips as much as she could, as if she could take him into her wetness without his cooperation.

"It would serve you right if I just took your mouth and left you wanting all day," he murmured, half under his breath, and Allison moaned, hoping he wouldn't do that. She'd go insane.

"Please, please, please," she begged, her back arching as he moved down her body and sucked her unabused nipple into his mouth, biting down on it hard enough to make her gasp. The attention to her breasts only made her even more aware of her empty, needy pussy. "I'll never wake you up with a blow job again."

"I didn't say *that*, Princess." Todd laughed, then bit down on her nipple again as he tweaked the other between his fingers, and Allison's body jerked. "In fact, I may insist on it every so often. The point is, you were trying to be sneaky, and you forgot I like to be in charge."

"Or I was counting on it," she retorted. Both of them knew he wasn't actually mad, and she had been trying to get into something just like this position, but half the fun of the game was pretending otherwise.

"Brat," he said fondly as his fingertips slid down her sides, and Allison writhed, trying not to giggle.

"No tickling!"

"Oh, I'm sorry, did I forget who's in charge here?" he purred as he walked his fingertips back up her sensitive sides, making Allison breathless with laughter.

At the same time, she couldn't have been more aware of the solid man holding down her lower body or the fact her legs were spread around his torso or the way he was moving back up her body until his cock was nudging her pussy again. His fingers found a particularly sensitive spot, and she gasped with laughter as her body contorted, and she kicked, unable to control her reactions, trying to buck him off. Allison *hated* being tickled.

"Hmm, I think we've found an effective punishment."

"Noooo!"

To her relief, Todd sat back, leaving her panting for breath, her body feeling sensitive from his devilish fingers. Allison glared at him, then tried to kick him again as he grabbed one of her ankles and spread it wide before attaching it to a cuff at the bottom of the bed. They'd chosen a four-poster bed for exactly that reason, and Todd had set up the cuffs on all four posters last night.

"You're going to regret that," he said, grabbing her other

kicking leg. Allison growled, and he laughed, admiring the sight she made so early in the morning—her arms restrained high above her head, her legs splayed wide open, so he could see her glistening pussy lips, and her breasts thrust toward the ceiling. It was a sight he'd seen before, but now they were in their own home, their bed, it seemed to have gained new significance. Now that both of her legs were restrained, he tickled the bottom of her foot, and she gasped and writhed, but she couldn't get her foot away.

"TODD!"

"Mmmm, I love to hear my name on your lips."

Her face contorted, and he could tell she was trying not to say something to him that would get her into *real* trouble. Truthfully, he didn't want that either. He'd much rather have a playful, enjoyable session of morning sex with her, but he had also really been enjoying the way she'd writhed under him while he tickled her right up until she'd started kicking. So, he got back in position over his glaring girlfriend, admiring her pretty hazel eyes, which were shooting daggers at him, and her parted lips just begging for a kiss… or a cock.

Kneeling between her thighs, he pressed his dick to her pussy lips as he ran his fingers up her sides again, enjoying her soft skin and the way she convulsed at his touch. Her pussy rubbed against the sensitive head of his dick as her breasts bobbled, and she tried to glare at him through her panting giggles. Once he reached her armpits, he quickly moved his hands away and pinched her nipples hard, knowing exactly how much she enjoyed having forceful stimulation applied to those sensitive buds.

Allison cried out, her body arching as her breasts thrust farther upward in an attempt to relieve the pressure, but he could practically feel her pussy gushing fluid to coat the head of his dick. With a low groan, he pushed partway into her, enjoying the snug, hot fit. Releasing her nipples, he let his fingers tease her sides again. Gasping and giggling, Allison writhed and struggled as he slowly sank his cock into her while continuing to torment her with tickling. He found it both extremely erotic and amusing, although she certainly wasn't the least bit amused, even if she was obviously aroused. Her pussy clamped and convulsed along with her body as he titillated her sides.

"Todd... please... stop!"

He could tell she was starting to truly gasp for breath, so he relented, wanting her to find the experience mostly enjoyable. Having a naked, helpless girlfriend, writhing on his cock was exactly how he wanted to start his day, and he didn't want to ruin that by pushing her too far—although he was definitely serious about using tickling as a punishment in the future if she required it.

Leaning over to capture one erect nipple in his mouth, he began fucking her in earnest. Allison wasn't sure if she loved or hated the tickling torture he'd just put her through, but she definitely hadn't expected it to be erotic. There had been something hot about writhing uncontrollably while bound, unable to stop him from literally doing anything he wanted with her body, even having him ignore her pleas had aroused her. When he'd started fucking while tickling her, it had taken her breath away, feeling him moving inside of her, so controlled and determined while she'd been completely out of control and at his mercy...

Now, she was writhing beneath him for an entirely different reason, still helpless and bound, spread wide open for his pleasure and hers.

Todd rode her hard, his groin slamming against her clit with every thrust, the little bud swelling larger as he rubbed against it. Arching beneath him, Allison reveled in her bondage, moving with him as much as possible as he slammed into her. As she gasped and began to undulate beneath him, her inner muscles clamping down on him as her legs pulled and twisted, Todd moved harder, faster. Feeling her cumming beneath him was driving him wild. Allison cried out with ecstasy as his thick cock forced its way into her spasming body, her pussy trying to clamp down on him, and her rapture only increasing as the rough friction continued.

He called out her name as he hunched his shoulders, using the leverage to split her open, moving relentlessly throughout his own orgasm to spur them both higher. With every thrust, he sent another spurt of cream deep into her body, both of them moaning with satisfaction as he filled her cunt.

Finally, he fell on top of her, his heavy body covering hers. Although it made it harder for her to breathe, she loved the feeling of his weight pressing down on her. His large body was warm, comforting, and having him pressed against her after an incredible morning orgasm seemed the perfect way to start the day.

"I think I'm going to like living with you," he said into her ear.

"You *think?*" Allison laughed. "Considering I'm all moved in, I think you'd *better!*"

Chuckling, Todd undid her restraints, which unfortunately meant removing his warmth from atop of her body. They wouldn't be able to wake up every morning like this once they were back to real life with work and school, but Allison comforted herself with the thought that some days, they'd be able to do this or something like it.

"I'm just making a projection into the future," he said, giving her a little slap on the butt as she started to roll out of bed. "But I don't *think* there will be a problem."

She tried to punch his shoulder, but he just laughed and swung around behind her again, giving her butt another love tap to start herding her toward the shower. Yeah, she could definitely get used to living like this.

"Whew," said Allison as she collapsed on the couch. "We're done!"

With a loud, overdramatic groan, Todd fell down on the couch, too—directly on top of her.

"Oof!" she pushed at him. "Get off me, you big lump!"

"Can't... too... tired... dying..."

Her fit of giggles didn't help with her efforts to dislodge him from her lap, neither did the fact he outweighed her by a good forty pounds of mostly muscle. Finally, she just accepted he was going to lie across her and fell back against the couch, laughing and enjoying his general silliness. While Todd could be so serious, so dominating sometimes, there were times when he was like a little kid, and she loved to see the boyish laughter in his face. He had so many conflicting sides to him, and she was enjoying uncovering them all.

One of the best parts about living together was uncovering each other's secrets, all the little things a person did when they were at home, comfortable, and felt like no one was looking. Although now, there was someone looking, Allison felt comfortable enough to let him see her do things like clip her toenails or tweeze her eyebrows. Some things she didn't do around him yet, but she knew eventually, they'd come. Every day she became a little more comfortable letting him see all the little things she'd be afraid to reveal to anyone else.

Like the mask she sometimes put on her face to help open up her pores. Or the fact she was terrified of touching raw meat—she picked it up out of the packaging with a fork to put it on the cutting board, sprinkled the spices on, then used that same fork to pop it into the pan. She knew it was weird but couldn't help herself. So far, he hadn't caught her doing that, but she knew eventually, he would, and while he would probably tease her, she felt pretty sure he would also love her for it.

Todd wriggled around on her lap until he was lying face-up, his head nestled on her legs, so she could stroke his dark hair. She loved to run it through her fingers, never tiring of the little intimacy that so clearly said he belonged to her.

"So... now we have furniture and basically a house... do we have a housewarming party?" he asked.

"Do you want one?"

"I just kind of assumed that's what people do. You know," he said teasingly, "your kind of people. Have people over, show off their stuff, accept gifts..."

Allison laughed. "You just want presents."

"And admiration. Lots of fawning compliments. Maybe a bit of jealousy."

"Silly man," she murmured, focusing her attention on smoothing her fingers through his hair. So thick and soft, she loved to play with it and try to mess it up, although all he had to do was run his hand through it, and it would fall back into place. "I don't know about a housewarming party, but I'd love to have Diana over, maybe Chad. Any of your friends you'd like to invite."

Todd raised his eyebrows. "Are Diana and Chad the only friends you have?"

"The only close ones I've had in a while," she said indifferently. She rarely found herself missing any of her old friends. Occasionally, Chrissy, but whenever they talked on the phone, it became more and more apparent, she and Chrissy weren't as close as they had once been. "I have some friends at work and some acquaintances through classes, but..." She shrugged. "I stopped talking to a lot of my old friends. We don't have much in common anymore. I don't really have time for more friends right now, anyway."

"I have a couple friends I wouldn't mind inviting. We'll keep it small. Four friends and they can each bring a date."

"Will I need to cook something?"

"A few things." He grinned up at her, tapping his finger on her nose. While Allison had slowly been learning to cook over the past year, she wasn't sure she was up to doing anything she'd be proud to serve at a party. "We're keeping it small and casual, remember? Nothing too fancy. And I'll grill. You can just do sides and dessert."

"Mmm, carrot sticks and instant mashed potatoes... yum!" They both laughed, and Todd pulled her face down for a kiss.

Allison couldn't remember the last time she'd been so happy.

Allison smiled as she looked around the rather successful party. It truly was casual, nothing like the parties her parents threw where she had played hostess. There was a distinct lack of judgment for one, and her new home was nothing like theirs, but she thought it had come out rather nicely. While she and Todd had resumed their usual schedules of work for him and work and school for her, they'd had time in the evenings to put a few final touches in place before the weekend, like the print of a painting on the wall in front of her. She'd stopped to study it on the way to the backyard, thinking how marvelous it was to have a print of a painting. Her parents would be apoplectic at the idea of not having the actual painting, but she rather liked it.

Especially because it wasn't an expensive print; she'd picked it up at BB&B, already framed, for thirty bucks. Another thing her parents would have had a fit over. She liked the man and woman dancing in the rain, the entire thing in black, white, and grey, except for the red dress the woman was wearing. When she looked at the painting, it made her think about love, but it also seemed like a comfortable, comforting piece. It reminded her it was the little things in life, like dancing in the rain, which were important.

Smiling happily, she turned her attention back to the party outside. Todd had invited a couple of friends, surprisingly, only one from his frat. The rest were from work. Brad and Chris, friends from work, had brought their wives, Wendy and Tina, and his frat buddy, Jake, had come alone. He and Chad were having a grand time, joking about forming a bachelor's club and arguing about whether Todd would qualify.

The big surprise guest of the day was Roger. When Diana had first called to ask Allison if she could bring him, she had at first hesitated bringing it up to Todd. After all, that was kind of awkward, wasn't it? Diana had insisted it wasn't necessary, she just wanted to ask, but Allison realized if Roger and Diana continued to date and she wanted to spend time with Diana, it would be best to set the tone now. Make sure Todd realized there was nothing romantic between them anymore, and that she didn't feel that hanging out with Roger was a big deal.

When she'd asked him about it, she thought that she'd seen a flicker of something in his eyes, but he'd readily agreed Diana could bring her boyfriend—even though he was Allison's ex. He knew Allison had never been in love with Roger, she'd reassured him of that, although she didn't bring it up again when asking if it was okay if Roger came to the party. Extra reassurance on top of what she'd already given him just seemed like making it a bigger issue than it needed to be, and he hadn't really seemed to need it.

So far, it hadn't been awkward, except Todd and Roger seemed to have disappeared. She'd gone inside to see if they were in the kitchen, but she couldn't find them anywhere. Returning outside, she scanned the yard. It wasn't like it was that big a yard. Pursing her lips, she wondered where they'd gone.

"I have to say, as great as this house is, I miss living with you." Coming up beside her, sipping on one of the fruity mixed drinks with colorful swirly straws Allison had provided, Diana managed to look simultaneously happy and pathetic, widening her eyes to increase the latter.

Allison grinned. "I miss living with you too. I'm glad you could make it today. Any idea where your man has wandered off to?"

"Somewhere with yours," Diana said, making a face. There was something in her expression that made Allison feel like her friend was hesitant to say more, which, for Diana, was extremely unusual. She was one of the most outspoken people Allison knew. It was one of the things that had attracted her to Diana as a friend.

"Do you know what they're talking about?"

"Unfortunately, yes." Stirring her swirly straw, Diana stared at her drink. The petite Asian was a pretty, confident, confrontational person, so Allison was surprised to see her looking so uncomfortable, which made her nervous as well. Before her own nerves could get the better of her, Diana sighed. "Your dad told Roger he should try to get back together with you."

"What?!"

"Yeah, I know," Diana said, rolling her eyes. There was both frustration and anger in her voice, probably as much on Allison's behalf as on her own. "Roger told him he had a new girlfriend, then your dad asked if Roger had a friend, he could set you up with."

"Unbelievable." Allison was fuming, though she wasn't really shocked or even all that surprised, just frustrated and annoyed. It was just like her parents to try to insert themselves into her life through someone else, now she wasn't talking to them, and who cares what she wanted. Then something else Diana had said caught her attention.

"Wait, so you guys are official now?"

Diana giggled and finally met Allison's eyes again. "Well, we weren't when he said that, but I guess now we are. I don't mind."

"And ah... is he everything you hoped he'd be?" Allison asked, teasingly referring to the talk she and Diana had had when Diana had first admitted she was interested in Roger. After watching Allison's relationship with Todd, Diana had finally realized she wanted a man who was more dominant in the bedroom, but for some reason, most of the guys she ended up with weren't. She would put up a challenge for dominance, and they would end up rolling over for her.

Dating Allison had definitely changed Roger, and while he wasn't who she wanted to be with, she hadn't been upset Diana was interested in him and wasn't that surprised he was willing to meet Diana's challenge. At least, she assumed he had since he was still around, and she knew that was what Diana wanted. After she'd broken it off with Roger, she'd seen him start to relax a little more from his usual gentlemanly demeanor, allowing some of the alpha male she'd always sensed in him to come to the fore. She suspected, deep down, he wanted it just as rough and dirty as she did, but she wasn't the person to show that to him because she didn't want it from him, she wanted it from Todd.

"Most of the time," said Diana. "He's not... you know, super arrogant like Todd, but he definitely doesn't let me take charge all the time. And if I try to push him toward something, he's not that interested in, I can't budge him, like most guys."

"Yeah, he's definitely not a pushover," Although the times when he'd resisted being pushed around by her had been when she was trying to push him away from his perceptions on how a gentleman and a lady behaved. Somehow, she didn't think that was quite the same as what Diana meant.

"I'm definitely expanding his horizons." Diana snickered, a rather wicked look on her face. Allison felt too awkward to ask for further details, but she could definitely guess. Diana was not shy about asking for what she wanted, and unlike when Allison had been dating Roger, she had no qualms about asking for things Roger might not consider 'proper.' When Allison had been with him, she'd been doing everything she could to be the perfect girlfriend, the perfect woman, and Roger had been all that was tender and gentlemanly. They'd both changed since then. She'd admitted what she really wanted, and she had a feeling Roger was starting to realize he had another side as well. There was no way Diana would make excuses for some of the requests she made as Allison had, when she'd realized how shocked Roger was at something as simple as wanting rough sex.

"Good." It was a little weird, her best friend was dating her ex, but she was happy Roger had found someone who suited him better, and Allison knew she was happier with Todd. "I just hope he told my dad he could go to hell."

"Uh... not in so many words." Diana laughed. "They do have to work together."

"Yeah, I know," Allison muttered. She wished someone *would* tell her Dad to go to hell. It would probably be good for him. Oh right, she'd already basically done that. It didn't seem to have made much of an impression.

Todd and Roger appeared in the backdoor, heading out to the porch. They were chatting amiably, but Allison could see tension in Todd's shoulders that hadn't been there before. Damnit, Roger must have told Todd what her father had said, not that it was going to change anything between her and Todd. She'd made her choice and was going to stick by it. Her parents were being ridiculous, cutting her out of their lives unless she lived her life the way they demanded —not going to happen.

Just looking at Todd and Roger, she could see the differences, and it was like confirming her decision all over again. Roger was definitely handsome, with his golden good looks and fit body, but he had a pampered air that can only come from an upbringing with money. He moved with an easy gracefulness, befitting a guy who had learned to fence when he was a teenager. In contrast, Todd was like a dark panther, his eyes holding a wariness of the world that came from having to fight for everything he'd achieved, and he moved like he was ready for another fight at any given moment.

When he looked over at her, she couldn't stop the smile that spread across her face. Just looking at him made her feel warm and tingly, even if she was feeling anxious. Todd smiled back at her, but she could tell it was an effort. The crinkling around his eyes and on his forehead said he was angry, and considering what a damn gentleman Roger was, she had a feeling he told Todd everything.

Shooting Roger a glare, she trotted over to where Todd was held up by Brad to chat and slipped her arm around his waist. Todd's arm curved around her shoulders, pulling her in close, so she could smell his slightly spicy, masculine scent and snuggle her head into the nook of his shoulder. Brad's wife, Wendy, gave Allison a little smile and snuggled closer to her own husband, sharing a look only women thoroughly content in their relationships could.

However much she might want to talk to Todd about whatever Roger had said to him, now was obviously not the time. Patience might not be one of her virtues, but it was occasionally necessary.

2

The rest of the party was enjoyable, although she had a small knot of tension in her stomach. Eventually, the party would end, and she would have to talk to Todd about what Roger said to him. In the meantime, it was fun to listen to him expound on his plans for the backyard to their friends, showing them where he wanted to put the pool and how he wanted to extend the patio. The guys seemed suitably impressed, and the women were excited by the idea of a backyard pool. They migrated inside and started playing pool on the table in the basement Todd had set up. The competition between Roger and Todd seemed a little more tense than usual, but playing on teams helped with that, and Allison didn't think anyone else had noticed.

Finally, everyone slowly trickled out the door. Diana and Roger left in the middle of the pack, which was a relief. She hadn't really talked to Roger all day, but decided she was okay with that. They were friendly, but considering her parents apparently wanted her to get back together with him, she definitely hadn't wanted to do anything that would make Todd or Diana feel insecure because there was no way that was going to happen. Before her conversation with Diana this afternoon, she wouldn't have worried, but since she knew it was likely to be a sore spot, thanks to her father, she'd decided not to rub at it.

Once they picked up everything outside, they moved inside. Todd stood at the sink doing the dishes as Allison cleared away the trash and started to put away the alcohol they'd set out, beers in the fridge, liquor in the pantry.

Examining the bottle of Jim Beam, she commented, "The Beams were not an attractive family."

"Probably why they started making alcohol," Todd said, flashing her his sexy smile. Allison giggled.

"Bourbon goggles. They explain so much!"

Todd looked mournfully at the picture on the bottle. "She was only a whiskey maker, but he loved her *still…*"

If it hadn't been for that little of emphasis, Allison might not have caught it. She gasped with horror. "You didn't."

"I don't know what you're talking about."

"We're going to have to set some ground rule for living together, Todd," she said warningly, glaring at him. "Rule number one—"

"Seems kind of late to set ground rules. You're already moved in, and we even had a party to prove it.

"No punning."

"I don't know what you're talking about," he said in his best innocent voice. "Pun? I never pun. Puns are the lowest form of humor."

"And your favorite." She didn't really mind, but she knew he enjoyed it when she gave him a hard time. Laughing was rarely an option unless it was accompanied by groans, so she just chastised him instead, and he adored it. She grinned back at him as she finished putting the alcohol away. They'd stocked up for the party, giving them a pretty good spread of whiskey, bourbon, vodka, rum, and liqueurs. Looking at all the bottles, most of which hadn't even been opened during the party, she shook her head, frowning. "This pantry makes us look like hardcore partiers."

Todd laughed. "Well, we won't drink it all at once."

"Oh, darn, and here I thought we were going to have one hell of a night."

Wiping his hands on a dishtowel, Todd walked over and slid his arms around her waist, pulling her hard against him. Allison grinned as she ran her hands over his chest, letting her head tip back, so her lips and face were turned up to him, eyes glittering with excitement.

"We don't need alcohol to have a hell of a night, Princess," Todd murmured as he feathered kisses over her forehead and down her cheek, moving toward her lips. She could feel her body tighten in anticipation. "In fact, the things I want to do to you, it's better if I haven't been drinking at all."

"Oh?" she asked archly. His lips pressed lightly against hers before moving away and kissing down the side of her neck. She tightened her grip on him, her body arching to press against him as the tingling sensation his lips created spread down her spine. "And what is it you want to do to me?"

"Let's go upstairs, and I'll tell you about it."

To her surprise, Todd didn't take her to their bedroom, but to one of the free rooms upstairs they hadn't decorated yet. They'd talked about making a few of the rooms into guest rooms or an office, but they hadn't agreed on this particular room yet. There was nothing in it at the moment, and the floors were hardwood with no padding. She really hoped he didn't want to christen this room today because it didn't seem like it would be very comfortable for either of them. Unless, of course, they used the wall...

Todd stood behind her, one hand splayed across her stomach, the other caressing her hip. Hot breath on the side of her neck, through her hair, made her shiver as she leaned back against him, her hands resting on the one he had on her stomach.

"So, I think I know what I want to do with this room," Todd whispered in her ear, his tongue flicking over her earlobe. Allison felt like she wanted to melt, as if she was putty in his hands. That had always seemed like a cliché, but as his hands moved over her body, inflaming her senses, she felt like she was something to be molded by him. Like she would sink down to the floor if it wasn't for his hands and arms holding her up, his long, hard body available for her to lean on. The bulge in his jeans pressed against her ass and lower back, and she rocked against him, enjoying the way his breath hitched.

"What do you want to do with it?" she asked in a husky voice. The emptiness of the room made their voices echo, even though they were speaking softly.

"I want to fill it with toys."

"For all the good girls and boys?"

"Well, for one girl who is not always good." Todd bit down on her sensitive earlobe, and she gasped, her muscles quivering as she went up on her toes. Her breasts thrust forward, and he squeezed one hard, his fingers searching for her nipple through the fabric of her shirt and bra. Allison shuddered as liquid heat traveled from her ear and breast straight to her pussy. She could feel her slick folds rubbing against the inside of her underwear as her restless movements caused the seam of her tight jeans to shift and slide against her. "And sometimes, is very bad."

She moaned. "I like that idea."

"Good. I'll start tomorrow, but after today, you're not allowed back in here until I bring you in. I want everything to be a surprise."

Todd turned Allison around and flipped her over his shoulder. If she hadn't been so turned on, she'd probably be laughing at his caveman-like behavior. Instead, as he carried her back to their bedroom, she worked her hands into the back of his pants and did her best to grab at his butt, enjoying the way his muscles flexed beneath her hands as he walked. There was something extremely appealing about being carried to the bedroom, even if this wasn't the most comfortable position to be in. At least the trip wasn't long.

With a low growl, he tossed her onto their bed and climbed on top of her, practically ripping her clothes off as he kissed and caressed her. A few buttons popped off his shirt as she yanked it, eager to get her hands on his skin. She'd learned to touch him as much as possible while she could because Todd definitely had a preference for restraining her, and her allotted time for getting her hands all over him was usually limited.

Grasping a breast in each hand, Todd allowed her to touch him as much as she wanted while he sucked and nibbled at her sensitive nipples, making her writhe beneath him and rub her crotch against his hard stomach. Digging her nails into his shoulders, she tried to pull him, indicating she wanted him to move upward, but Todd ignored her signals and continued to lavish attention on her breasts, biting down on her nipples hard enough, Allison cried out as the exquisite pain lanced through her, making her pussy cream even harder.

Latching onto the side of her breast, and he sucked hard, his teeth digging in. It was a completely different sensation from the hard suckling of her nipples, but just as pleasurable. Allison moaned and ran her fingers through his hair, teasing his ears with her fingernails. She wanted to lean forward, to kiss him or tease his ears with her tongue, but the way Todd had them situated, it was impossible.

His mouth left behind a dark bruise on the side of her breast, then moved to the other, latching on almost viciously, his teeth digging into her soft flesh. As she keened wordlessly in reaction to the erotic pain, one hand pressed between her legs, his fingers sliding between her wet folds as the heel of his palm rocked against her swollen clit. Allison grabbed his hair, gasping as three fingers thrust hard into her, roughly stretching her as Todd left his mark on her tender skin.

Dimly, she remembered the last time he had left hickeys all over her was when he'd come home to find out she was dating Roger. He was marking her as his own. They hadn't talked about what her father had said to Roger yet, but Todd was making his feelings about the subject quite clear with the dark red bruises blooming like flowers on her breasts. His fingers curled, finding that sweet spot of sensation, and she moaned as all thoughts were swept away by the tide of hot need that bloomed from her center.

"Todd... oh, fuck...."

Todd's mouth left her breasts and covered her lips, a demanding kiss that ate her breath and made her jaw ache with its force. His fingers pumped inside her, his thigh pressing against the back of his hand as he rocked the heel of his palm harder against her. Gripping the hair at the base of his skull, her fingers digging into his neck, Allison kissed him back with all her passion and love, doing what she could with her body to show him she wanted him and only him. Everything he was doing was about more than love. It was an animalistic need to mark his territory, to confirm she was *his* woman.

Knowing he would never act upon his jealousy outside of the bedroom or do anything to stifle her friendship with Roger, Allison gloried in this private claiming. Feeling the kind of emotion, even the thought of living without her could rouse in him, was a heady experience. She loved the possessive way his hands moved over her, his mouth sucking her skin, the way he purposefully moved to drive her absolutely wild. There was an urgency to his movements, spurred on by his need to claim her all over again.

The thick rod of his erection pressed against her thigh, his fingers thrusting hard inside her until she felt as if she might explode. She sucked his tongue into her mouth almost frantically, her body arching as her nails skidded down his shoulders and back. As the pleasure culminated, her cunt tightening down on the wriggling fingers inside her, Allison cried out in ecstasy, the sound muffled by Todd's mouth. The heel of his palm rocked against her clit, grinding into the small bud, and she writhed with the intense sensations pulsing through her.

He drank in her moans and cries as she rode his hand until her movements slowed, and the death grip she had on his shoulders relaxed. The pressure of his hand against her clit lessened, although he continued to move his hand and fingers in slow, circular movements, coaxing the last shudders of her orgasm. Allison moaned softly as their kiss became less demanding, more gentle. Lassitude seemed to spread through her body in the wake of her climax, making her feel as though she might sink into the bed.

Leaving her lips swollen and well kissed, Todd began to work his way down her body, not sucking as hard on her flesh this time around. Looking down as he kissed his way down her stomach, Allison could see the vivid bruises on her breasts, the slight imprint of teeth around a few of them, which turned her on even more. There was something erotic about seeing his imprint and knowing he'd been out of control enough to leave teeth impressions, not just love bruises. As his mouth reached her hips, his fingers began to slide out of her pussy.

"Spread your legs more, Princess, and put your feet flat on the bed." The husky gravel in Todd's voice made her shiver. When his fingers slid from her pussy, she felt empty, and she wanted him back inside her.

The new position spread her completely open for him, exposing all of her most vulnerable parts to his eyes, hands, and mouth. Todd kissed her bare mound as one finger, soaked in her pussy juices, pressed against her asshole. She whimpered as he worked his finger into her tight back door, stretching the crinkled hole as each small thrust pushed his digit deeper. The wonderful full feeling was accompanied by his tongue sliding up her pussy folds, lapping the orgasmic juices from her climax. Gasping, Allison reached down and grabbed his hair, feeling torn between pulling him away and trying to pull him farther into her. Her pussy was very sensitive, the soft licks of Todd's tongue almost rasping over the swollen flesh.

"Todd... oh, fuck... it's too much!" Her thighs tried to close around his head to stop the delicious sensations coursing through her oversensitive nerves. Ignoring her, Todd used one hand to spread open her right leg, the other one curling uselessly over his shoulder as he began to force a second finger into her clenching anus, his tongue circling her clit. The myriad of sensations had her gasping and undulating, her hips bucking into his mouth despite her protests. "Oh God... Todd... you can't.... oh, fuuuuuck..."

The fingers in her ass pushed deep, buried all the way to his knuckles as they probed her tight hole, lubed only with the cream from her pussy. More juices ran into the crack, further lubricating his fingers as he pumped them in and out, the wicked sensation making her pussy spasm emptily. Todd worked his tongue into her needy hole as Allison clutched his hair, moaning and thrashing as she tried to gain some control over the situation, but he easily ignored her efforts and did what he wanted to her body, which only served to inflame her further.

Her free leg, the one he wasn't holding, kicked out, connecting with nothing but air as he sucked her clit into his mouth. The slow, gentle suction coiled tension deep in her pussy, the fingers in her ass adding to the heat. Todd's thumb slid easily into her sopping cunt, and Allison keened as her breasts thrust upward, her lower body speared on his fingers, and her most sensitive scrap of flesh securely lodged between his lips. His tongue flicked over that tiny bundle of nerves as he increased the suction, and Allison writhed, her legs spreading open of their own accord as the instincts of her body took over, and her need to cum again spiraled higher.

The fingers in her ass spread, and Allison's head fell back as the tight hole was stretched farther, her inner muscles clamping down hard as the first tingling tremors of her orgasm rippled through her. As if Todd could read her mind, the suction on her clit increased almost unbearably as his tongue flicked and rubbed the engorged nub. Allison screamed and writhed as a second orgasm wracked her body, even more intense than the previous one. Dimly, she knew her legs were curling over Todd's shoulders as if she was trying to drag him further into her pussy, her hands were gripping his head, and her hips were working up and down, but all of these actions felt separate and distant from the overwhelming ecstasy ripping through her.

Her clit throbbed in his mouth, juices spilling from her cunt down the crack and lubricating the fingers pillaging her ass, slickening that hole even more as it quivered around the invading digits. Todd gently released her clit, licking it with long broad strokes as Allison shuddered out the last of her orgasm. Her entire lower body felt overheated, swollen, and tingly. She whimpered with each stroke of Todd's tongue, each thrust of his fingers, every one of her muscles watery and overworked.

Relaxing her grip on his hair, Allison let her hands rest on his head. Almost despairingly, she wondered how she was going to be able to handle any more sexual activity. Her body felt overused, as if she might burst if she wasn't allowed to rest. To her surprise, Todd got off of the bed and reached over into a drawer full of goodies. She whimpered as he pulled out a long, bumpy vibrator.

"Noooo..."

Allison tried to make her muscles cooperate to escape, but Todd was on top of her again before she could move. His cock nudged the entrance of her swollen, sopping vagina, but she knew it wasn't anything more than a tease. He wasn't going to fuck her now, he was going to play with her some more. There was no other reason to bring out the toy. She didn't need more foreplay, she was ready, wanting, *needing...* right now!

"Yes, Princess," he murmured as he thrust his hips forward. Allison gasped and quivered as he speared her in one smooth stroke, her eyelids fluttering as his cock pushed aside the walls of her cunt with its thick girth, stretching her so wonderfully and yet so brutally, considering her sensitive nerves, it hurt and she found herself trying to push him away.

Grabbing her hands, Todd secured her wrists in his and held them above her head. The power in his body compared to her weak and watery muscles was so arousing, her cunt shuddered around his cock even as she thought she couldn't possibly take anymore.

"Please, Todd," she pleaded, her body wriggling under his, her pussy contracting around the thick length of his dick as he held it inside her. He was hard as steel, and her pleas were only turning him on more. They both liked it when she struggled, but on occasion, he liked to push her to the point, she was truly struggling against him and completely overwhelm her with too much pleasure until she fought him. "It's too much... just fuck me, please. Just fuck me and cum."

"Oh, Princess," he murmured, lowering his lips to her neck, loving the way she trembled beneath him as he brushed his lips along too-sensitive skin. "Since when have I ever 'just fucked' you?"

He pulled his wet cock out of her pussy and angled his body to the side, allowing him to slide the vibrator deep into her body. Allison jerked as he flicked the switch, and it began to pulse inside of her.

"Noooo," she moaned, her pussy clamping around the toy in instinctive reaction. Todd let go of her wrists and hooked her legs with each of his arms, pushing them over his shoulder as he lined his cock up with her winking asshole. The tiny, crinkled entrance slowly spread as the mushroom head of his cock pressed against it. When she brought her hands up to push him, Todd grabbed her wrists, one in each hand, and held them down to the bed as he leaned forward, pressing his body further into hers and bending her in half.

As his cock sank into the hot, velvet grip of her asshole, Allison seriously thought she might die from the overload of pleasure. The sensation of his rubbing against the long vibrator in her pussy, separated only by a thin membrane, and the overly stuffed feeling of being plugged in both holes was almost more than she could bear in her sensitized state. Weakened by the long day and two previous orgasms, Allison struggled against him, more of a token protest than anything else. It was obvious she wasn't going to be able to stop him from having his way with her, and part of her didn't want to, anyway.

She loved every way Todd dominated her—whether she obeyed him immediately, was punished for disobeying, or was forced into submission, her body craved it. As his cock buried itself into her protesting asshole, burrowing deeper, despite the clenching ring of muscle that seemed desperate to push him out, Allison realized she was going to cum again—soon. She fought against the orgasm as Todd began to ravage her asshole, thrusting hard and fast, taking her breath away as he opened her straining anus. Every hard thrust pushed the vibrator deeper into her pussy, so he was fucking her with twin poles.

"Oh, fuck... oh, Fuck... OH, FUCK...." Allison barely recognized her own voice as she screamed, tears forced from her eyes as the avalanche of her orgasm overtook her, her overstimulated body snapping with intense explosions. As she came, she writhed and struggled, bucking beneath Todd as he pounded her into the mattress, his cock spearing her ass through its clenching grip.

Having her so wild beneath him, so out of control and under his domination, combined with the long wait he'd given himself, was too much for Todd, and he cried out as he thrust deep into her asshole. Her tight hole clenched around the base of his cock so hard, it was almost like a cock ring as his cum forced its way up the length of his dick into her spasming ass, filling it with hot liquid.

The throbbing rod in her ass provided no final relief for Allison as the vibrator hummed in her pussy, fully inserted, and she continued to wail and gyrate. Tears trickled down the sides of her face, and she thought she saw sparking black and white lights as her body tightened and released, over and over again. Even after he released one of her wrists and slid the vibrator from her shuddering cunt, Allison's body twitched and shivered.

Todd helped slide one of her legs over to the side, so he could maneuver them into a spooning position. Allison whimpered and shuddered as he curled behind her, the soft cushion of her ass cheeks pressing against his groin. Kissing the back of her neck, Todd wrapped one arm under her head and the other over her stomach, holding her tightly against him.

They laid like that for long, silent minutes. Allison was in a hazy, dreamlike state, although she wasn't asleep quite yet. She liked to stay awake for as long as possible when she and Todd cuddled, enjoying the warm, hard length of his body against hers. Especially on nights like tonight when he took her in her more private opening. They had anal sex on a regular basis, but not nearly as often as they had regular sex, and there was still something so incredibly intimate about having him take her there.

"Roger said your dad wants you to get back together with him," Todd said finally, breathing the words so softly into her ear, if she had been asleep, he wouldn't have woken her.

"Fortunately, my dad doesn't get what he wants when it comes to me anymore," she murmured. Not quite as quietly as Todd since, after all, he was behind her, and she wanted to make sure he heard her. His arm over her stomach tightened, acknowledging her words. "I don't want Roger back. I chose you."

"You haven't talked to your family since you argued with them about me."

Allison shrugged with the shoulder that wasn't on the bed. "And I don't plan to. Not unless they reach out to me."

"Don't you think that this might have been their way of reaching out?"

She gave an exasperated sigh. "If they're going to 'reach out' through my *ex* and say they want me to get back together with him, rather than contacting me and apologizing for caring more about their social status than they care about me, I don't count that as 'reaching out.'"

In fact, she found it hurtful, selfish, snobbish, childish, and not something she would respond to. It was insulting to Todd as well, and she took that even more poorly than she did the insult to herself. All they had done was stoke her anger all over again and made her even less inclined to yield.

There was a long quiet moment as Todd stroked her stomach, his face buried in her hair. She could feel his breath on the back of her neck, and she snuggled back closer, putting her arm over his, curving it over her stomach.

"I don't want you to never talk to your family again. Not because of me."

"It's not because of you," she protested, squeezing his hand. "It's because of me and them. Because I'm not doing what they want."

"But you're not doing what they want because of me."

The silence between them lengthened. This was not the way Allison thought tonight was going to go, and it frightened her to think Todd might draw away from her under some noble idea of sacrificing himself, so her parents would talk to her again.

"Even if it weren't for you, I wouldn't have stayed with Roger. I wasn't happy with him. I'm happy with you. I'm living with you, and I want to live with you. My parents were already upset about a lot of things in my life—like the fact I was working and had moved out. Trying to regulate my dating life was just the last straw. It's not you, it's them. And the fact I've grown up and didn't want them running my life anymore."

Todd didn't say anything, and Allison felt new tears spark in her eyes, responding to the aching feeling in her heart.

"I'm not leaving," she said in a low, fierce voice. "I'm not leaving, and even if you kicked me out, I wouldn't go back to my parents or to Roger. I want *you*."

That startled a laugh out of Todd, and the bands around Allison's chest relaxed.

"I'm not going to kick you out," he said, holding her tighter, if that was even possible. She wriggled back against him, encouraging the attempt to get even closer. "I was just thinking, maybe you should try talking to them again, that's all."

"I'm not going to them, they can come to me," she replied a little hotly. "They're the ones acting ridiculous."

"You could give them a demonstration on how to act, be the bigger person and make the first step," he said, although there was now a tone of amusement in his voice.

She shook her head. "That will just make them feel as though they're right."

"Not if you stick to what you want. Then it will just show them you still want to talk and try to work things out."

Stroking the back of his arm, Allison played with the dark hairs, trying to make them stand straight up as she thought. While she did miss her parents because they were her parents, she wasn't sure she was ready to make the first move. After all, her father was the one who had pretty much kicked her out of their house, telling her she wasn't welcome back until she was ready to let him dictate her love life. Her mother never went against what her father said. Both of them cared too much about appearances and their own social climbing and not enough about her.

Part of her felt if they really loved her, they would realize she should be allowed to live her own life—work if she wanted to work and date who she wanted to date—whether or not they approved. Told she had to live by her father's dictates or be unwelcome in their house, made her feel as though she wasn't loved by them at all. And the idea she should have to approach them first, risking confirmation of their lack of love, risking a second round of rejection... Well, she wasn't sure she could handle that. If they came to her first, she would know they were putting her before their pride and social status.

But she didn't want Todd to feel like he was the cause of the rift because he truly wasn't. Possibly, he was a symbol of how she was going to decide things for herself, but he definitely wasn't the entire reason.

"I'll think about it," she said finally.

He gave her a hard, little squeeze, as if he wanted her to know he appreciated the compromise, but he wasn't entirely pleased she wasn't immediately taking her suggestion.

Unlike her parents, however, he didn't reject her, just held her tight as they fell silent and finally drifted to sleep.

Three days after the housewarming party, Allison was in the school library when her mom called. Of course, since her phone was on silent, she didn't know until she left the library after finishing her research and took out her phone to turn the volume back on. Chewing her lip, she stared at the missed call and voice-mail notifications.

Part of her dared to hope, maybe her mom was calling to make a peace offering. The sinking sensation in her stomach was her more pessimistic side disagreeing. She should have expected this, really. After all, her parents had told her straight out, they wanted her to get back together with Roger. Then they'd gone to work on him. Now, it was time for the follow-up.

Almost a standard business model. A straight-on hit, followed by one from the side, then the follow-up. Best to send in the more sympathetic party—i.e., her mother. Wouldn't do for her father to show himself backing down. A kind of familial good cop/bad cop, with a side of heavy manipulation.

Getting into her car, she decided to let the engine warm up while she listened to the message. Spring was coming, so was gradu-ation, and she was looking forward to both. While she liked cold weather at first, she was always ready for it to start warming up by the time it finally did. She would also be happy to be finished with school, so she could just work full time instead of splitting her time between work and classes. Especially since then, her evenings would be completely free to spend with Todd rather than doing homework.

Tightening her lips, she tried not to get her hopes up too much as she dialed her voicemail and put in her password.

"Hello, Allison." Her mother's elegant tones resounded in her ear, managing to sound concerned and cool—the sound of home. "I was hoping to hear from you before this, but since you haven't called... Your father and I know you saw Roger this past weekend and hoped you might have some... news for us. We miss you, sweetheart. We hope you make the appropriate decision, and we'll see you soon." The words cut through Allison like knives, but the biggest cut of all came as pleading entered her mother's voice. "Come home soon, dearest... We love you. I want my daughter back... please..."

Guilt and fury fought for space in Allison's emotions as her mother hung up, and the voicemail asked if she wanted to delete or save the message. She saved it, wiping away the treacherous tears at the corners of her eyes. The last bit of her mother's message was so emotional, not at all cool or elegant, as if she truly did miss Allison and wanted her back. Yet... the love her mother spoke of, that welcome back, was obviously conditional on her acquiesce to her parent's expectations. Her mother wouldn't even say Todd's name or reference she was in a relationship already, much less that Roger was. Did they not know about Roger and Diana? Or did they simply not care? Allison found it all too easy to believe both scenarios.

3

_____

When Todd came home that night, Allison was busy baking. The kitchen was warm from all the use the oven had been put to, and there were several trays of baked goods on the kitchen island. She was decorating sugar cookies with home-made icing while she waited for her salted caramel butter bars to be done. Fortunately, for both her and Todd's waistlines, it was easy to get rid of baked goods. All she had to do was take them into work, and it was like vultures descending on a feast.

She'd come a long way from the days when she'd made chocolate chip cookies to help her relax. While she didn't consider herself a great cook or baker, she'd learned a lot, and enjoyed trying out new recipes—especially on days like today when she was upset. The more she thought about her mother's voicemail, the more upset she got. Considering how much her mother said 'we,' her father obviously knew her mother was calling, although he wouldn't lower himself to talk to the daughter he'd cast out until she was back under his thumb.

Further incensing her was the complete lack of regard for anyone's desires other than their own. Somehow, she couldn't see Roger hiding his new relationship from her father, he was far too honorable and honest, which meant her father knew, even if her mother didn't, and at least one of them just didn't care. The absolute disregard for anyone's lives but their own made her furious, and she'd worked out that emotion, kneading bread. In fact, she'd gone a little overboard kneading the bread, and it hadn't come out very well, but at least she'd felt better after pounding the poor dough for almost an hour—until her arms were too tired to do anymore.

The fact her parents were trying to tempt her back into their fold with the promise of their love, rather than just loving and accepting her for who she was, was the worst part. *Yes, we will love you, but only if you do what we say.* That hurt the worst. Despite how they were treating her, Allison still loved her parents unconditionally, the way it was supposed to be. She kept telling herself they didn't mean it the way it sounded, but that's how it felt right now. Especially since she didn't feel like her arguments were particularly convincing.

Standing in the doorway to the kitchen, Todd looked damn good in his black suit, crisp white shirt, and the red patterned tie he was loosening from around his neck. Eyeing her almost warily, he draped his jacket and tie over the back of the couch before sitting at one of the stools at the island, next to a tray of pinwheel cookies. Poking at one, he found it was warm but not hot and picked it up as Allison gave him a little smile. She set down the cookie she was icing and picked up the next one.

"So, what's wrong?" he asked.

It was useless to pretend nothing was. Even if she hadn't told him about her penchant for baking when she was upset, Todd could read her like a book. The sheer amount of baked goods would probably tip off a much less observant man.

"My mom called today and left a message." There was an art to icing cookies. You had to hold the cookie just right, so it didn't crumble between your fingers, putting just the right amount of pressure on the knife, so it didn't break any pieces off, angling it just so to make the icing look its best. Almost two dozen cookies in, Allison was getting pretty good at it. "Wanted to know if I'm back together with Roger yet. If I am, they'll love me again."

Todd grabbed her hand as she set the cookie down before she could pick up another one.

"That's not what she said."

"Close enough." Allison blinked to keep away the tears that threatened. She refused to cry over her parents' intransigent attitude anymore. Talk about useless tears. He squeezed her hand, rubbing his thumb over her knuckles. Allison clenched her jaw and met his eyes squarely. "It's fine. I'm just angry all over again."

He wanted to tell her, of course, her parents loved her, despite the way they were acting, but understandably, he didn't think she would react well to that right now. Instead, he just stood and walked around to her side of the island, releasing her hand, so she could keep icing cookies, put his arms around her waist, and hugged her close. After a moment, Allison relaxed, sinking back against him, so her body molded to his, her movements slowing as she iced the cookie she was holding.

"Want to go out to dinner?" he asked. "We can come back here for dessert." The blandness in his tone was more mocking than if he'd actually pointed out the giant spread of sweets she'd made.

Allison giggled, little more cheerful now that Todd was home and gently teasing her. Just being held by him was wonderful, knowing he loved her and wanted to make her happy. She was especially happy he wasn't going to push the whole contacting her parents' thing. Although she didn't think he could be any happier about the fact they wanted her to get back together with Roger than she was, she knew he was stubborn enough to not let go of the idea, she should make the first move toward reconciling with her parents.

"Yeah, that sounds nice," she said, putting down the cookie and icing knife. "I can finish these later."

"I'm going to go change into something more comfortable," he said, turning her around with his hands on her hips. Leaning down, he kissed her deeply, passionately. Allison pressed against him, her tongue sliding against his. When he pulled away, he dropped a light kiss on her nose before heading upstairs.

It was amazing how just a few minutes with Todd could change her entire mood. she covered the icing and finished cookies with plastic wrap, then piled the unfinished ones in a Tupperware container. Just as she was finishing, the timer went off for the salted caramel butter bars. Taking them out of the oven, she set the pan down on a wire cooling tray, then headed to the bathroom to wash her hands and put on some makeup. She rarely wore any when she went to school, although she still wore it on days she worked. Todd liked the natural look on her, but she couldn't get over the urge to put some on when they went out. Was it something left over from her mother or just a girl thing?

She limited herself to eyeliner, lip gloss, and a light dusting of brown shadow on her eyelids, keeping the natural look, just enhancing her features a little. The eyeliner especially helped to make her eyes really pop. When she went into their bedroom, Todd was sitting on the bed, putting on his sneakers. He was wearing a pair of dark blue jeans that hugged his legs and a deep green shirt with the sleeves rolled up and secured with a small band of fabric that buttoned onto the shoulder—casual but sexy.

Looking down at her own outfit, she disappeared into the closet

"What are you doing?" Todd called out from behind her.

"I just want to change my shirt." She'd been wearing the same thing all day. She was wearing a plain red long-sleeved t-shirt, and while it hugged her curves nicely, she definitely didn't feel like she looked as good as Todd did. Examining her options, she grabbed a black, purple, and grey Asian-inspired blouse with a V-neck and bell sleeves. It only took her a moment to change, and when she walked out of the closet, she was glad she had as Todd's eyes glittered appreciatively.

Sitting on the bed, he was completely ready to go, his hands clasped and hanging between his knees. He opened his arms so she could stand between his knees with her hands on his shoulders. Leaning over, she kissed him gently as his hands slid up the backs of her thighs and gripped her ass, then slid around to the front of her hips and gently pushed her back.

"You'd better stop that, or we're not going to get anywhere tonight," he warned.

"Ohhh... okay," she said with a little giggle as she turned away, then yelped when he gave her butt a sharp smack.

Grabbing her ankle boots, she quickly put them on, and they headed out the door.

~

O ver the next few weeks, Allison wondered if her parent's desires had had more of an effect on Todd than she'd thought. He was acting particularly affectionate. He'd always been demonstrative, but it seemed like even in private, he was going out of his way to touch and cuddle her... and she reveled in it. They watched movies cuddled up on the couch, played footsie while they played Scrabble, and held hands everywhere they went. Some of it was a little distracting, like the back massages when she was trying to do homework, but she wasn't going to complain.

There was a special softness in his eyes every time he looked at her. It was enough to make her wonder if he was already thinking about the next step in their relationship beyond living together. Not they'd been living together for very long, but they'd settled in very quickly. Both of them were easy to live with, happy to change their patterns to accommodate the other. It helped they both were generally neat and clean people, although it was already becoming obvious, Allison was a little messier than Todd, mostly when it came to leaving clothing around the house. He'd bought a second laundry hamper to put in their bathroom. Otherwise, she just left her clothes on the floor until they piled up enough for her to notice, then she'd put them in the basket in their bedroom.

"Have you looked?" Diana asked when Allison shared her thoughts.

They were in Allison and Todd's kitchen, cooking dinner. Todd had to work late, so Allison had invited Diana over to hang out and help her make dinner. It kept her from being alone and also meant she got to catch up on her girl time. She missed having dinners with Diana now they weren't living together. Living with a girlfriend was completely different from living with her boyfriend. Not in a bad way, but she did miss some of the benefits of living with a girl—like gossip time.

"Looked for what?" Allison stirred the zucchini, trying to make sure each slice cooked evenly. Not exactly easy since the pieces kept flipping on top of each other. The pan was slightly too small for them to be laid out in a single layer of zucchini slices. They were almost ready for the parmesan cheese.

The kitchen smelled delicious. Diana was stirring the 'home-made' spaghetti sauce, she'd created by taking a jar of Prego and adding red wine and extra spices. Slowly stirring it, she occasionally tested the flavor. She'd insisted on wearing an apron over her casual blue shirt and dress slacks, not so much that she was worried about getting it dirty but because she liked wearing an apron when she cooked. Breaded chicken, stuffed with mozzarella was baking in the oven, adding to the wonderful aromas. Home cooking at its best as far as Allison was concerned. Tasty, but most of all, easy.

"An engagement ring."

"What?"

Diana rolled her eyes as she tasted the spaghetti sauce, dipping her finger into some of the sauce on the spoon she'd been using to stir.

"Have you looked around to see if he's bought an engagement ring? Then you'd know."

"I mean... it's just a feeling. He hasn't said or hinted at anything... it's just... this idea I get in my head sometimes lately. Not really enough to go snooping around for a ring."

"You don't need more than that to just *look*," Diana said persuasively. Allison bumped her hip playfully against Diana's as she lowered the heat on the zucchini and began sprinkling parmesan cheese on the slices. The cheese didn't need much heat to melt, and it would burn pretty quickly if the pan was too hot.

"Let's say I'm right... he obviously wants it to be a surprise, and I shouldn't look," Allison said. "If I'm wrong, there's nothing to find, anyway." She turned off the heat on the zucchini now that the parm had melted just a bit. Yum. "Is the sauce ready?"

"Yeah." Diana glanced at the timer sitting on the counter to her left. "We have ten minutes left before the chicken's ready."

"That's okay, it just means the cheese on the zucchini will melt a little more."

"Good," said Diana cheerfully as she turned the heat on the sauce down to simmer. She flashed Allison a wicked little look. "That gives us time to search!"

"Wait!" squealed Allison, laughing and following as Diana took off, not even bothering to remove her apron. "You don't even know where to look!"

"Always start with the bedroom."

Amused, Allison followed Diana up to the bedroom, watching as her friend quickly went through Todd's drawers. She didn't do anything more than feel around for a jewelry box, so it wasn't quite as invasive as it could be. Then Diana moved onto the closet, but unless Todd was hiding it in his shoes, there wasn't anything there to find. Allison didn't think it'd be in the bedroom. She went through Todd's drawers too often. She had a penchant for wearing his t-shirts around the house.... and his sweatpants. They were more comfortable than her own, and she liked the possessively pleased look he got when he saw her wearing his clothes.

"Have you done this before?" Allison asked as she watched Diana peek into the drawers around Todd's computer in the study. "You seem to have a bit of a system."

"Oh, my parents used to hide Christmas and birthday gifts in all sorts of places," Diana said as she closed the last of the drawers and tapped her fingers thoughtfully on the computer desk. "I definitely haven't searched Roger's place like this, if that's what you're asking. We're not at that point yet."

"Do you think things might go there?" Allison was genuinely curious. So far, she and Diana hadn't talked much about Diana and Roger's relationship. Sometimes, she wondered if Diana felt it would be too awkward, but she seemed completely casual about dropping that nugget of information.

"Maybe. He's the first guy I've ever dated I could see myself considering taking that step with." Standing in the middle of the study with her hands on her hips, Diana examined the room as if a hidden compartment with a ring box might suddenly jump out at her.

Allison put her hand over her mouth to cover her smile. It was funny that Diana was more interested in this search than Allison was, but truthfully, she was happy with what she had at the moment. Maybe eventually she'd want to get married... but it wasn't at the top of her list of priorities right now, not when she was concentrating on graduating in a couple of months.

"Is there anywhere else in this house that's just Todd's?"

"Ummm..." The toy room he was creating sprang to mind. Allison had honored her promise not to enter it, so if Todd was going to hide something in the house, that would probably be the best place. She had no idea what was in there. He sometimes received large packages in the mail or brought things home wrapped, so she didn't know what was going in there. Curiosity had almost gotten the better of her a few times, but she liked surprises. Plus, he'd probably blister her bottom for ruining this particular surprise.

"Where?" asked Diana immediately.

"Well... he's setting up a room for us to ah... play in," Allison said a little hesitantly. She knew Diana wouldn't judge her for whatever Todd had in there, that wasn't the problem. The problem was she was tempted to send Diana in there, even though that would definitely be pushing the boundaries of following Todd's orders. Still, it would technically be obeying him since she'd only said she would stay out of there. Nothing had been said about other people or friends. "I'm not supposed to go in there until he's completed it."

Diana's face lit up. "Oooh, that sounds promising! Where is it?"

"The room across the hall."

Diana scooted out of the office with Allison following close behind. As Diana turned the doorknob, Allison positioned herself next to the door frame, facing the opposite side of the hall, so she wouldn't even be able to see inside.

"What are you doing?" Diana gave her a strange look. "Don't you want to see what's in here?"

She rolled her eyes. "Of course, I do, but Todd told me not to look. I'm pushing it by letting you go in there."

"You're such a goody-goody sometimes," Diana teased as she practically pranced into the room. "Oh, holy crap!"

The unfeigned awe in her voice nearly broke Allison's resolve not to look.

"What?"

"I'm not going to tell you." Diana giggled. "After all, this *is* supposed to be a surprise. Damn. Now, *this* is a sex room. Hmm... here's some drawers... Maybe there's a ring in here.... Oh, my..."

Now Allison was pretty sure Diana was saying things just to get a reaction from her. Although there was also honest delight and surprise in her voice, so maybe there were some really *good* goodies in there. Shifting foot to foot, Allison reminded herself she would eventually get to see everything in there. More than see—she'd be using everything in there.

Faint insistent beeping downstairs sounded down the hall, just as she heard the front door open.

"Diana! Todd's home! Get out of there!" she hissed before rushing down the stairs, heading for the kitchen. Todd home and the chicken ready—well, at least her timing when it came to cooking was getting better. She could hear Diana following her down the stairs.

Todd stood in the entryway, looking up at them with amusement.

"Hello," she said with forced cheerfulness. "Dinner's ready! Perfect timing!"

She gave him a quick, hard kiss before rushing away to the kitchen, hoping he didn't see her guilt. Diana engaged him in conversation, hopefully distracting him. The damned man was usually way too good at reading Allison's emotions for her comfort, especially in situations like this, where she was feeling too flustered to cover up anything she didn't want him to see. Diana managed to keep him from coming into the kitchen long enough for Allison to get herself under control and start filling up the plates with dinner.

It was a fun meal once she managed to get her heart rate under control. Despite the fact Diana still had the urge to constantly prod Todd, trying to get reactions from him, the two of them had worked out a pretty amicable friendship. In fact, they acted more like siblings than anything else, with Diana in the part of the annoying younger sister, who wanted to get her brother's attention. No set-down ever kept her down for long.

Todd told them about a new project he was assigned at work. He wasn't in charge, but he was the second in command, and the guy who *was* in charge was acting more as a mentor than a lead. Her heart swelled with pride as she listened, knowing exactly how hard he'd worked to get into this kind of position. Even if some of the details were incredibly boring, she thought it was really cute how excited he got about all of it and knew it was a really great opportunity for him, showing upper management, he was ready to move on to bigger and better things within the company.

Since she was only working part-time, Allison had hit the ceiling for how far she could go in her own position, which was okay because she wasn't sure she wanted to stay in Human Resources. It was great experience, but she'd really prefer to do something in communications. Not like Todd did, with his flair for marketing, but something like writing out the explanation of someone else's ideas or copy-editing.

Fortunately, that was something she didn't really need to decide until closer to graduation, although she would be putting in applications before she was done with school. Todd had suggested it, and she thought it was a good idea. Although she'd like at least a week between the end of school and starting a new job, it definitely didn't hurt to try to get a jump on things.

After dinner, he offered to do the dishes, but Allison and Diana sent him upstairs since he'd already had a long day of work and hadn't had a chance to change out of his clothes. Plus, it gave them more of a chance to continue their own whispered conversation under the cover of running water and clinking dishes. Tonight, more than once, Allison had seen that *look* in his eye and wanted to know if Diana had seen it, too.

"Allison."

Todd's deep voice, laced with more than a hint of steel punctured the air. Even though he hadn't spoken loudly, there was a great deal of menace in his tone. Allison shut off the water and turned to face him. He only used that particular tone when she'd done something wrong, and when she turned and saw the expression on his face, she *knew* he knew. She just didn't know how.

"Yes?" she asked, her voice wavering.

For once, the irrepressible Diana seemed to be unsure of what to do. She shifted her weight next to Allison, shooting little glances at Todd, the way a gazelle might look at a lion on a faraway hill, wondering if the lion was hungry and if running would make one safer or just attract attention.

"Would you like to explain to me why the door to our... ah... special room was left open?"

She couldn't help it. Even though she wasn't trying to pass the blame, she glared at Diana. Seriously?!

Diana winced. "Sorry." She looked at Todd. "Allison didn't go into the sex room, just me."

Rolling his eyes as if asking for patience from the heavens, Todd let out a sigh, but Allison also saw his mouth twitch when Diana called it a 'sex room.'

"Following the letter of the law if not the spirit. Why am I not surprised?" It was amazing how Todd could make her feel like a naughty little girl with just a look. Allison bit her lip and shifted from side to side. "Stay here." Turning on his heel, Todd walked from the kitchen, his stride worryingly purposeful.

Allison and Diana shared a look.

"What do you think he's doing?" Diana whispered, actually sounding worried. Considering how curious she'd been about the room, Allison had a feeling the best punishment Todd could have devised was not letting Diana know what was going through his head. Unfortunately, she didn't have any better idea than Diana did. She'd never seen Todd react quite that way.

"I have no idea. Come on, let's finish the dishes." Maybe being industrious would give her a bit of a reprieve.

The little Asian suddenly scowled as she helped Allison with the dishes.

"He'd better not think he can do anything *me* just because he spanks you. Roger would throw a fit."

Despite herself, Allison felt a stab of jealousy at the idea of Todd punishing Diana.

"Does Roger spank you?"

To her surprise, Diana's cheeks got a little red. With her slightly darker skin, that meant she was *really* blushing.

"Once or twice."

"Did you like it?"

"Yes." Diana looked over her shoulder to make sure Todd wasn't there to overhear. "Although he's nowhere near as rough with me as you've told me Todd is with you. But I think he might be headed that way, eventually… He *really* liked it."

"At least he's doing it at all." Allison was having trouble picturing gentle, loving Roger as a disciplinarian. Sure, he'd shown flashes of wanting something rougher, of being a dominant alpha male when they were together, but he'd been fighting against that part of himself. While she realized he must have changed a little in his new relationship—because that's what Diana wanted and she wouldn't have stayed in it otherwise—Allison was still having trouble picturing him doing it. On the other hand, that was probably for the best. She wasn't entirely sure she wanted to picture what Roger and Diana got up to in the bedroom.

Silence fell over the kitchen as they finished the dishes, each lost in their own thoughts. Diana kept nervously glancing toward the doorway where Todd had disappeared as if she doubted whether or not he might punish her. For herself, Allison was pretty sure Diana wasn't in trouble with Todd, although she was and had no doubt, whatever discipline he chose, it would be creative.

When Todd finally strode back into the kitchen, both girls were more than a little on edge. If he had meant to make them suffer by waiting for the blow to fall, he'd definitely achieved that. Diana looked even more anxious than Allison felt—it was pretty obvious, she wasn't very used to waiting for *anything*.

A smug smile curved his lips as he looked at Diana. "I hope you don't mind, Diana, but I'd like some quality time with just Allison this evening. Also, Roger is expecting you at his place within the next half hour."

Diana's jaw dropped, and she gaped at him. "What?"

"Roger is expecting you at his place." Leaning casually against the kitchen island, Todd resembled a cat toying with a mouse, it wasn't particularly interested in eating, only tormenting. "I believe he wants to have a... chat with you about respecting other people's privacy." His dark eyes seemed to pin Diana, and Allison watched with fascination as her friend's cheeks turned an even darker red. Todd glanced at his watch, then gave her a wicked grin. "I would hurry if I were you, I don't think you'd want to add tardiness to the things he wants to talk to you about."

Looking both excited and uneasy, Diana allowed herself to be ushered from the house, giving Allison a quick hug as she went out the door.

"Sorry," she whispered in Allison's ear as she hugged her.

"It's okay," Allison whispered back. "I could have stopped you."

Rather than apologizing to Todd, Diana just tilted her head back and gave him a particularly unrepentant look. Of course, her haughtiness was ruined by the way she then swiftly hurried to her car.

Watching Diana flee with an amused smile on his face, Todd slowly closed the door as the taillights of her car receded before turning to Allison. His dark gaze was filled with a wicked glee that made her want to back away slowly. As much as she might enjoy rough sex and being spanked, that didn't mean it didn't sometimes *hurt*, especially when Todd was disciplining her.

"Let's go upstairs," he said in a low voice, anticipation thrumming through it. "There's something I'm ready to show you."

4
─────────

"*S*how" ended up being more subjective than literal.

The asshole blindfolded her before taking her into the room. Talk about a punishment! She was in the room and could feel the cool smoothness of the hardwood floor, but she couldn't see a damned thing. Other than the blindfold, she was completely naked. Todd had stripped her down outside the door before putting the blindfold on her and told her she was never allowed to wear any clothes in this room unless he told her to.

She didn't need her eyes to know it was a sex room—filled with who knows what. Well, Diana knew.

That bitch.

Allison wasn't truly angry, just envious. If she'd known she was going to be punished anyway, she might have taken a peek. Then again, perhaps that would have just netted her a worse punishment. Although being in the room and still not being able to see it was pretty bad. As much as she tried to cast her eyes downward, she couldn't see anything past the edge of the blindfold other than a dim sliver of light. Not exactly informative.

Todd led her to where he wanted her, then put her hands on something smoothly padded and inclined downward.

"There's a place for you to kneel. Don't worry, I'll help you."

He guided her into a kneeling position, then made a few adjustments of machinery before pressing her upper body down. The incline was fairly gradual, but it left her ass high in the air. Her stomach was supported, and there was a section that seemed to be cut out purely to accommodate her breasts, so they hung straight down. There was something supporting her forehead, almost like a massage table, so her neck didn't strain. Despite the basic comfort of the apparatus, there was something extremely intimidating about the position. All of her most vulnerable parts were more than exposed—they were presented like an offering. As if to accentuate that point, Todd's caressed her butt cheeks.

"Lovely, Princess."

He secured leather straps, one around each thigh, another around each calf, one around each wrist that secured her to hand-holds for her to grip, and one around her waist, leaving her completely vulnerable to whatever he was going to do to her. Allison was shaking with trepidation, and she didn't need Todd's finger sliding up the center of her slit to know she was soaking wet in anticipation.

"You have no idea how gorgeous you look," Todd murmured, both of his hands gripping her ass hard and spreading the cheeks apart. Allison moaned as his tongue delved into her wet pussy, but the restraints prevented her from moving her hips even the slightest bit to encourage him. All she could do was take whatever he was willing to give her, which apparently was a lot of teasing. His tongue never approached her clit, although he licked and nibbled at her pussy lips before licking his way around her crinkled asshole and teasing the delicate nerves centered there.

"Oh, please..." She started to beg. The ache in her pussy to be filled or even just to have him flick her clit was becoming unbearable. She could cum with the smallest bit of encouragement, yet Todd seemed determined not to let her have that. Instead, his tongue just pressed inside her hungry cunt. She struggled against the restraints, trying to wiggle herself back into his mouth, to no avail. "Todd, please... touch me... I'm so close..."

With a long sigh, Todd released his hold on her cheeks and pulled away from her pussy. "As much as I love hearing you beg, Princess, I can't exactly call this punishment."

She let out a noise halfway between a mewl and a growl. "Well, I would."

The sharp slap on her pussy sent a shudder rippling through her... God, she was so close to cumming, but the slap had been so unexpected, it didn't quite push her over the edge.

"I think that's enough talking from you. You may moan, scream cry... but no words, or I'll add to your punishment."

His hand unexpectedly slapped down on her swollen pussy lips again, and her entire body convulsed. Damn this blindfold! Allison wriggled against the restraints, but Todd had obviously known what he was about when he secured her. No matter how she tried to move, she couldn't. The only real movement as she wriggled was in her breasts, which jiggled enticingly on either side of the apparatus she was bound to.

Squeezing her right breast, he kneaded it, pinching and tugging on the nipple. The image of a cow being milked flitted through her head, and if she wasn't so desperately turned on, she might have giggled. Once her nipple was plumply erect, something bit into it, and she gasped as the harsh pain flitted through her straight to her needy pussy, which clenched emptily as she groaned and attempted to breathe through the sharp bite. Todd moved around her, heading to her other side, to her other breast, but the pinching sensation didn't ease, and she knew he had clamped her.

Now that she knew what was coming, it was harder to relax into the caresses on her breast, but her left nipple hardened as readily as her right, and the rubber clamp bit into it just as sharply. Both nipples throbbed in time with each other as the blood flowing into the tender buds was stymied. Fingers trailed to her lower back, making her skin tingle but not quite enough to distract her from the pain in her breasts. Nipple clamps were always what Allison thought of when she used the phrase 'hurt so good.'

Todd's tongue laved over her asshole again as if putting her on notice, it was going to receive special attention. Her buttocks flexed in anticipation.

"I have a new toy I want to try." The eagerness in his voice caused rising anxiety in her, considering her situation. "I was going to save the cane for a time when you needed discipline. I didn't expect to get to use it so soon." The excitement in his voice rose. "Since it's your first time, I'll only do five strokes."

A cane? Some part of her felt as if she should be panicked—the things she'd read online said canes were supposed to hurt a *lot*—but right now, she craved the pain and was curious what it would feel like. The sharp bite in her nipples made her want a corresponding bite on her lower body, and if Todd wanted to use a cane, she wasn't going to protest. Not that protesting would have done much good.

Sometimes, she wondered how far into depravity she would follow him, but so far, he'd never done anything to her she hadn't ultimately enjoyed. He'd told her if she ever said "red," he would stop immediately, but Allison had privately vowed never to use it. She loved when he pushed her, loved giving up her control to him and enduring whatever he chose to dole out. The pain became her own private pleasure, eventually sending her soaring to heights of ecstasy, she'd never known were possible.

The reverie of remembered pleasure was brutally interrupted by a whistling sound and a shocking pain across her ass. It didn't hurt the way Todd's hand or even a paddle or whip, it *burned* and stung, a thin line of tortured flesh marked across her creamy buttocks. Allison shrieked, her fingers closing hard on the handgrips. Her buttocks clenched and released, her body striving to find an escape from the humming torment. She was supposed to let him do that *five* times?

He caressed her bottom, his palm pressing against the line he'd made across her creamy flesh. It felt hot against his hand, and Todd smiled, enjoying the sight of Allison truly struggling with a punishment. The cane was something he wanted to use very rarely, so he had decided to make this first punishment with it particularly memorable. Her firm buttocks had clenched the moment he touched her and remained so.

"Relax your buttocks, Princess," he murmured. There was a muffled sob, then Allison shook her head, following his dictate not to speak. He gave her ass a slap, but it didn't have the same kind of impact as when her cheeks were relaxed—which, of course, was why he wanted her to unclench before he gave her another stroke of the cane. Beneath his hand, her bottom trembled but didn't unclench. A wicked grin spread across his face. There was something else he'd wanted to try.

To Allison's surprise, Todd didn't bring the cane down on her bottom again. Apparently, he wanted her muscles relaxed before he did, but Allison didn't want to relax her muscles. She didn't want another stroke of the cane—not yet. When she was ready to go through that again, *then* she'd relax.

Todd moved around her, but she couldn't figure out what he was doing. He hadn't left the room, and it sounded like he'd opened and closed a fridge. Was there one of those up here?

"I understand this is new to you," he said in a low, confident voice, approaching her from the front. Allison's muscles tensed all over again. She was even more vulnerable than before, and she hadn't known that was possible. "But when I tell you to do something, you will do it immediately, or you will suffer the consequences. I have something that will do two things—punish you for not relaxing your muscles when I told you to and help you strive to relax those muscles."

He walked around her, moving to her backside. The stripe across her bottom still burned, and all the jiggling had pinched her nipples even more, although that small pain seemed to have subsided a bit. She wasn't sure if it was because her nipples were slowly numbing or the pain of the cane stroke was so much more intense, by comparison, the clamps didn't get as much attention from her brain.

Something cold, wet, and firm pressed against her asshole. By now, Allison had learned it was best to relax her muscles when Todd wanted to insert something in her ass, to keep from feeling undue pain. Her bottom automatically unclenched, and she shivered as the cold object slid inside her. There *must* be some kind of fridge in the room for something to be that cold. It felt long and much thinner than she expected and strangely fleshy. Despite the cold liquid on it, it didn't seem to be very lubricated, and she groaned as Todd worked it back and forth, pushing it deeper inside. Her anus expanded over a bump, then closed, just as it would for a butt plug, although this didn't feel like any plug she'd ever experienced.

"In Victorian times, caning was quite often used as a punishment," Todd said conversationally from behind her, not touching her now that whatever he had put in her ass was inserted to his satisfaction. "But the effectiveness of caning is less when the subject's muscles are clenched, so they used this little technique to encourage the subject to relax their bottom."

He touched the little thing inside her, and it jiggled. Allison automatically clenched, wondering what he was talking about since so far, it didn't seem to be doing anything at all. Her asshole felt a little tingly, but that was it. Todd's voice lowered, becoming a sadistic caress as he explained exactly what was going to happen.

"It's ginger. Soon, it will start to burn. You're going to try to relax your asshole to stop the burning, but you won't be able to help it when the cane strikes. You're going to be burning and stinging inside and out, but the more you can relax, the less it will hurt."

The tingling had increased to a stinging burn, and she was starting to have trouble concentrating on his words. They turned her on but at the same time, terrified her. Instinctively, she knew he was going to push her boundaries again today, right now. The burning flared, feeling as if her asshole was on fire.

"Please... oh God... Todd, it hurts!" she cried out as she started to writhe, fighting against the restraints.

Instead of responding, he laid another stripe across her bottom with the cane, now that her butt cheeks were relaxed as she'd tried to escape the burn of the ginger. Allison shrieked as her back tried to arch, the restraints doing their job of holding her tightly in place. Just as he'd explained, the burning stroke across her cheeks made her clench them, and she cried out again as the burning pain increased. She truly was burning inside and out.

Rather than making her wait, Todd brought the cane down

quickly, barely giving her time to breathe between strokes, laying the third one down two inches below the second. Watching her fight and writhe only turned him on more. He grasped his cock in one hand, fisting it as he tried to hold his own desires in check. The lines across her bottom stood out starkly red against her ivory skin, the little finger of ginger moving slightly in her bottom as she clenched and unclenched her muscles, wailing with the burning pain. Beneath her marked ass, her pussy was pouting, swollen and red. Ginger also had an aphrodisiacal effect, one which was becoming quite clear as her juices coated her inner pussy lips and the tops of her inner thighs. Her clit was an erect red button, having pushed its way out from its hood, begging for attention.

He landed the fourth stripe just above the sensitive crease between her bottom and thighs, saving that particular area for some later punishment—a larger infraction. By now, Allison was rocking back and forth, unable to escape either the burning of the ginger or the sting of the cane. Being blindfolded only made the sensations seem more intense, her focus on listening for the whistling sound that heralded the next shocking impact and on the burning torment of her lower body.

The last stroke came down on a diagonal, crossing all four of the previous strokes, and Allison screamed. It was the worst one yet, reigniting every other stroke. If her limbs hadn't been restrained, she would be thrashing from the sexual torture. The ginger burned and throbbed in her ass as Todd massaged her butt cheeks, rubbing his hand roughly over the marks he'd laid down on the blank canvas of her ass and making Allison writhe and cry out as his hands sparked a whole new kind of pain as her flesh pulled and moved.

When he carefully pulled the finger of ginger from her ass, she almost sobbed with relief, although the tormented hole still tingled and stung. She only had a moment of relief before Todd was pulling the clamps from her nipples. Blood rushed into the pinched buds, and she cried out as her body focused on this new source of distress. Her body was being absorbed by erotic anguish, all of her sexual organs throbbing with the agony Todd had elicited.

Suddenly, his cock was sliding into her, hard and merciless, splitting her shocked vagina wide open. Until the moment he entered her, she hadn't known she was wet. Slick with juices, her pussy had been creaming throughout the torture, despite the pain. Being filled by his thick cock felt good—right—as if this experience wouldn't have been complete without the sexual invasion of her body.

His groin bounced off of her brutalized ass cheeks, and she moaned fitfully, her pussy spasming around him as the pain and pleasure slammed against each other like lightning into water, mixing and filling her with shimmering electricity that sparked the nerves throughout her body. There was no moving away from his rough strokes, his grasping hands as they kneaded her buttocks and pinched her nipples, or from the ecstasy rising inside her, so close, yet she had no control over when it would encompass her. She was a vessel, held immobile to receive his cock and his cum.

As he pistoned in and out of her, fucking her hard and relentlessly, Allison's tender asshole and pussy spasmed, the walls of her cunt rippling over his turgid length. The angle the apparatus held her gave Todd a terrific amount of leverage to abuse her body, his hands hard on her hips. Every slap of his body against hers, reignited a flaring pain across the welts the cane had made as his balls smacked against her swollen clit.

"Fuck... Allison..." Todd's breathing was getting heavy as her body tightened around him, the sheer eroticism of having her so tightly bound before him, of tormenting her reluctant body, obviously having its effect on his usual stamina.

With the blindfold over her eyes, Allison's world narrowed to a kind of tunnel vision, focused entirely on the cock fucking her raw. The searing pain in her ass had subsided after he'd removed the ginger, down to a tingling, which only made her body more hungry for the orgasm building in her core. As if the release of tension would also completely soothe the burn from the ginger.

"Oh God..." Her voice came out in a gasp as Todd's pace increased, every thrust sending her ecstasy cresting higher as if he was building her orgasm like a pile of blocks until he kicked it, and she shattered. Allison howled as she fell into pieces, her body attempting to curl, to spasm, to retreat as Todd fucked her hard, sparking waves of pleasure that rolled through her as implacably as an ocean wave.

Her body shaking with the overwhelming sensations, she was lost in a maelstrom where pain and pleasure had ceased to have meaning. Her passion smothered her intellect as she keened and shook, an animal of lust and rapture, a slave to Todd's erotically twisted desires. The darkness behind the blindfold seemed to flash bright white, sparking with bursts of glittering white flame. She screamed as his fingers dug hard into her hips, and he crashed into her from behind. Inside of her, his cock throbbed, swelled, and burst forth, filling her with a hot gush of fluid.

Every pulse, every spurt, her body spasmed in response, sucking his cum deep into her body.

As he gave a few last, slow thrusts, wringing the last of his orgasm into her cunt, Allison whimpered and moaned. She was exhausted, trembling, and for the first time, she was truly glad of the restraints because she felt quite sure she would have fallen off without them. Fully inserted inside her, Todd made soothing noises as he stroked her back, feeling her muscles relaxing beneath him after the arduous session he'd just put her through.

Todd's stroking fingers calmed her, and she felt like she was wrapped in cotton, her mind muzzy as if she was surrounded by white noise. While she could hear the low tone of his voice and feel comforted by it, the individual words didn't penetrate the fog in her brain. Dimly, she was aware of the restraints around her body falling away and Todd's arms wrapping and lifting her.

Reality seemed to slip away, her mind numbing as her eyes closed. Sensation ruled—smooth, hard flesh, wiry hair against her cheek, gentle fingers on her side, the coolness of the air brushing along her skin.

Time became meaningless, and the next thing she knew, she was sinking into heat, steam rising from the water. Strong arms held her safe and secure around her middle. A sudden flare of pain as she settled into the bottom of the tub, the marks on her ass burning. She writhed, but her weak muscles were no match for the hands pushing her back down into the water.

"Shhh," a soft voice murmured into her ear. "It will only hurt for a moment, then it will help."

As if she had no control over her muscles, she still struggled weakly against the arms that were like steel bars around her waist until the stinging faded, along with her resistance. The heat enveloped her, pulling her down. The water smelled like lavender and was gentle against her skin, now that it was no longer stinging the welts across her buttocks. Todd cradled her, holding her head above water, and gently rubbed down her limbs with a washcloth.

She was limp, although the relaxing bath actually seemed to be refreshing her, as well as relaxing her. As he rubbed the soapy cloth over her breasts and stomach, she was slowly waking up under his ministrations. Despite the tenderness of his hands as he washed her, her beaded nipples were still very sore from the clamps, and she whimpered a little as he handled her.

"Good girl." The whisper of his voice across her ear made her shiver almost as delightfully as being called a good girl. While in some circumstances, she might find it patronizing, coming from Todd, it always made her feel flush with pleasure as if it was the greatest accolade she could receive.

Twisting around slightly, she tipped her lips up toward his for a kiss. She caught a flash of amused dark eyes before his mouth slanted over hers hungrily. As much as she'd enjoyed the position he'd put her in for discipline, she wished kissing had been possible. She loved kissing Todd. He tasted like warmth and sexy man, his tongue delving into her mouth as though he was just as eager to taste her. The cloth in his hand rubbed over her stomach and hips as his other arm slid upward, tucking itself under her breast as he pulled her further into him, lifting her slightly to make it easier to devour her lips.

Trapped by his arms, Allison couldn't touch him the way she wanted. She rubbed her hands over the arm beneath her breasts, sliding through the hair on his forearm, wriggling back against him as if she could push herself farther into his body. The slick glide of his muscles against her back, lubricated by the water, felt wonderfully sensual.

Todd's chest rumbled as he broke off the kiss with a small laugh. "I'm trying to wash you, Princess."

"I'm not stopping you," she said, giving him a little smile to go along with the wiggle of her hips.

"You have no idea how distracting you are." He kissed the tip of her nose before nudging her, so she turned around again, her back resting against his broad chest, her head falling back onto his shoulder. Allison let out a happy little sigh as he began to rub her with the soapy cloth again. "Insatiable, aren't you?"

"Only for you." Closing her eyes, Allison turned her head into his neck, luxuriating in the warmth of the bath, the tender care in Todd's hands, and the comfort of giving herself over to his pampering.

"Are you going to open the door to that room without again?" he asked.

"Not until you tell me I can," she said, her voice fervent and felt the rumble of his suppressed laugh through his chest. As one hand pushed the washcloth down to her shaved mound, the other gently caressed her breast. Despite the softness of his touch, a little zing of sensation went through her nipples, causing her to shudder. It wasn't pain exactly, but a sensation that walked that thin line. Her nipples were too sore for it to feel entirely good, yet Todd's touch was too sensually delicate for it to be bad.

The rough washcloth rubbed over her tender pussy lips, stimulating the nerves there. Allison shuddered and moaned, her hands coming to rest on Todd's strong thighs, placed on either side of her legs, allowing him full access to her body. This was an entirely different kind of sexual experience compared to their session in the sex room. He was making love to her with nothing more than his hands and soft kisses along her hairline.

Her breath caught as he began a ceaseless, coaxing rubbing between her legs, taking her bruised flesh and filling it with pleasure. Allison's back arched, her hips moving with his clever fingers, the nubby fabric of the cloth giving her entirely new sensations.

"Cum for me, Princess," Todd said as he nuzzled her head to the side before sucking her sensitive earlobe between his lips and nibbling on it. Allison moaned as the gentle waves of her orgasm lapped at her, her toes curling as the delicious sensations rippled through her. It was a much softer climax, yet even more intimate. He stroked her through the very end of her pleasure, then resumed his gentle washing as lassitude overtook her.

By the time he carried her to bed, she was practically asleep in his arms, completely sated from their activities. Todd curled around her, tucking her smaller body into his own as he smiled into her hair.

"I love you, Princess," he said into the darkness.

5
---

*A*lmost a month later, Allison still hadn't seen the sex room.

Of course, she'd also been behaving herself, and considering how much the caning had hurt, she wasn't sure she wanted to go back into the room. Apparently, one blindfolded session in there had been enough to give Todd more ideas about things he wanted to do in the room before he let her see it. Sometimes, she could hear him working on wood and metal in there, constructing who knows what.

She probably would have been more curious, but it was time for mid-terms. As an English major, she didn't have midterm exams, but she had papers due, and writing a paper took her a lot more time than studying for an exam. Although she had to study for two exams as well. Students were discouraged from taking more than three English classes during any given semester due to the amount of reading and writing involved. So, she still had to study for her science and her history exams and had to write a short paper for history as well.

It didn't give her a lot of time to ponder the sex room. Besides, Todd was more than inventive in their own bedroom, so she was completely satisfied. Even after she was done with her midterm papers, her thoughts mostly turned toward graduation.

Graduation was constantly on her mind for a myriad of reasons. The biggest one wasn't that she'd soon be done with school. It was a reluctant desire to call her parents and see if they could make up. She hadn't heard from them since that message from her mother, which meant they knew she was still with Todd and not back together with Roger, although she saw Roger occasionally since he was dating Diana. Since Todd had called Roger to let him know Diana had snooped through things she had no business snooping through, the two men had struck up a cautious friendship and seemed to be becoming more comfortable with each other.

It helped that Roger was obviously smitten with Diana, and Todd could tell Allison was happy about that. There had never been a high amount of sexual tension between Allison and Roger when they were dating, and now their relationship had settled into an easy-going, platonic friendship. They would hug a greeting or a farewell, occasionally touch if they were passing each other, but there was no way for anyone to misconstrue their actions. They just didn't have that kind of chemistry between them. Whereas, whenever Allison looked at Todd, she would get all tingly and excited.

The look in Roger's eyes when he was with Diana was something she'd never seen before, and Diana was happier than Allison had ever seen her, although she tended to view Todd with suspicion. Apparently, he'd started giving Roger a few pointers on keeping Diana in line. For the first time, Allison had the treat of seeing Diana a bit on edge in a relationship, the same edge Allison constantly felt she was walking. It was fun to tease the guys, but go just an inch too far, and they risked finding themselves draped over a masculine thigh with their bare butts in the air.

The relationships were making everyone happy except Allison's parents. She couldn't believe they still hadn't come around. Despite everything, she'd thought they'd want to see her graduate. Even if they didn't think she needed a degree, it seemed like the kind of milestone parents wouldn't miss. At least, caring parents wouldn't miss it. And not hearing from them as the end of the school year loomed closer, convinced her more and more, they didn't care.

As if he could sense her distraction and depression, Todd was making a major effort to spend a lot of time with her. Not just going out, but also spending time at home watching movies or playing board games, spending time with friends. And, of course, engaging in hot, rough, wild sex whenever he could get his hands on her. She was enjoying her work, doing well in school, loved her friends, and Todd was everything she could ask for in a live-in boyfriend. Truly, her parents were the only negative spot in her life.

Ruthlessly, she pushed all thoughts of them aside. She was getting ready for a date with Todd—a fancy date, which they didn't do often because they both preferred casual, but every once in a while, it was fun to get all dolled up like she used to on a regular basis and go out to dinner. Then come back home and have Todd divest her of all of her high-class finery and use her like the wanton slut she was for him.

Tonight, she was wearing a new dress he insisted she get, and she'd decided to go all out. At first glance, it was a rather demure dress, still sexy but very covering. A deep purple color, the dress was made of a very fine, very soft material that clung to her curves, helped by the broad belt covered with dark gems that cinched her waist. The dress wasn't a true wrap dress, although the top and bottom resembled one, with the fabric overlaying itself to create a v neckline and a small V at the center of her thighs—easy to slip a hand into. The bra she'd chosen pressed her breasts up, lifting and plumping them to create a nice cleavage. She'd wrapped the strand of black gems, which matched the gems on the belt, once around her slender throat, so the end dipped into the valley of her breasts, drawing attention to the assets which were almost entirely covered, yet impossible to ignore.

Her eye shadow matched the dark purple of her dress, and the color made her hazel eyes stand out even more, contrasting with and heightening the amberish color. Long lashes blinked slowly as she examined herself in the mirror, looking for any stray hairs that might have escaped her messy updo. Messiness by design was good, actual hair escaping where she didn't want it was not. No blush was necessary, her cheeks were already flushed with excitement.

Going out to dinner with Todd was usually accompanied by some bit of naughtiness, and he always managed to surprise her. Sometimes, it would be something that presaged the date, such as a plug in her ass or a vibrating thong, sometimes, it was something as simple as being fingered to orgasm while she at her dessert, but he always did something, and it was always extremely enjoyable.

Since he hadn't indicated he'd be dressing her in any kind of panties, she was wearing a lacy black thong that matched her bra, knowing he loved the way her creamy skin looked as it peeked through the lace.

"Are you almost ready?" she heard him call from the bedroom.

"Almost," she called back as she gave herself a sultry look in the mirror. She'd locked him out of the bathroom, not wanting him to see the preparations for the final product. It was more fun to knock him over with the full effect.

Sitting down on the toilet, she slid her feet into the strappy, glittery black heels, she'd bought to go with the dress. They were three inches high, which would put her close to his height, easy enough for her to walk in for as long as she wanted, and would show off her calves to their best effect. The kind of shoes that made a woman feel sexy, no matter what else she was wearing, although considering how good she looked tonight, Allison didn't actually *need* the extra boost of confidence, but the shoes went damn well with the dress.

Giving herself one last look in the mirror, a smug little twist to her lips, Allison strutted out of the room. Todd was sitting on the edge of the bed, leaning over to tie one of his shoes. So, he hadn't been quite ready yet, either. He was drool-worthy, wearing a suit she hadn't seen before, a dark charcoal grey, almost black but not quite, and that bit of lightness made his black hair seem even darker. The crisp white shirt beneath highlighted his dark good looks, and a lighter grey tie with a silver clip with delicately scrolled engravings, a very antique-y look, completed his suit.

Allison's breath caught in her throat as he turned his head, his gaze starting at her strappy footwear, traveling up her legs and over her curves to meet her eyes, hungrily drinking her in. Lust was written in every line of his face, but there was something else—something indefinably *more*. It was the same look she'd seen in his eyes more and more the past few weeks, as if his emotions for her had become so strong, he couldn't look at her without them spilling over. Was that normal? It was that look which had made her wonder if he was already thinking about moving their relationship to the next level, but so far, nothing had happened despite there being plenty of opportune moments. She'd convinced herself to stop looking for something, she wasn't even sure was coming.

With a definitive jerking movement, Todd tightened the laces on his shoes and slowly sat up, never taking his eyes from her. A slow smile curved his lips as he stood, the kind of smile that made her shiver and wonder if they were actually going to make it out the door.

"You look delicious, Princess." The tone in his voice filled the words with extra meaning.

She liked to play the game as much as he did, but it was more fun if she made him work for it. Arching an eyebrow, she shifted her weight, so one hip gently thrust out, making the material around her curves tighten. His eyes dropped to the contours of her body, drinking in the seductive invitation.

"You don't look half bad yourself," she purred, sliding one hand over her hip and up to her waist, her fingers delicately curving around the narrowest part of her body. Her blood thrummed, and she giddily wondered if she *could* keep him from their reservation. Todd was always so controlled, it might be fun to try.

But he dashed that notion. She could almost see him reining in his passion, making the conscious choice to wait for later—to make *her* wait. Truth be told, he was much better at drawing out the tension and extending the wait than she was. He smiled, holding out his hand to her, and she stepped forward to slip her fingers into his palm, loving the warmth of his hand around hers, the strength of him. Smiling up at him, she understood the expression, "swept away by love."

During the drive, she began to get suspicious.

Five minutes before they arrived at their destination, she was silently arguing with herself over whether he actually would.

He had.

When he pulled into the parking lot, Allison burst out laughing, and Todd slanted her a look, although he was grinning.

"That's not exactly the reaction I was going for."

"We're a little overdressed, don't you think?" she asked between fits of giggles. She'd had all sorts of visions in her head of what kind of fancy restaurant he might be taking her to. Not that this restaurant wasn't nice, but they would definitely be dressed at a much higher level than anyone else.

Todd batted his eyes at her, feigning innocence as he pulled into a parking space, but the glitter of amusement was unmistakable.

"Are we?"

"You know we are," she said, unsnapping her seat belt and leaning forward to grab him by the collar and pull him into a passionate kiss. Really, he was too cute for words. Getting her all dressed up, so he could surprise her and take her back to the restaurant where they'd had their first real 'date.' Granted, she hadn't entirely appreciated the gesture at the time—he *had* been blackmailing her—but she'd found it wonderfully exciting and appreciated it a lot more later.

This gesture, she appreciated completely. It heightened her anticipation, making her hope for... things...

Don't get ahead of yourself.

A romantic evening did not automatically mean a proposal. Just taking her back to this restaurant was incredibly lovely in and of itself. She felt incredibly special and giddy he'd gone to the effort of making it a surprise. She pulled away from the kiss, trying to put all of her appreciation for him, her love, into her eyes as they gazed at each other. Todd leaned forward and brushed another kiss across her lips before he unclipped his own seat belt, and they got out of the car.

"I don't mind being overdressed," he murmured as he took her hand in his, walking toward the front entrance. "Do you?"

"Not at all," she said, beaming up at him and wrapping her free hand around his elbow. When she felt all floaty and happy like this, it was all she could do to keep herself from wrapping all sorts of body parts around him, wanting to touch him as much as possible. He definitely didn't seem to mind. They were both walking with a little extra spring in their steps.

As soon as they arrived, the maître d' welcomed them, grabbed two menus, and led them to the same secluded booth they had been in before. The restaurant had quite a few people in it, but there was no one in their little corner and no way to see what was going on in the booth until you were standing almost directly in front of it.

Sliding into the booth, Allison gave Todd a flirtatious look, leaning into his shoulder as the maître d' gave them the day's specials, then disappeared. The conversations around them were a muted hum, and Allison was thrilled with the privacy. It was possibly the best thing about this restaurant.

"Does this count as romantic?" Allison asked playfully, bumping her shoulder against his. Todd laughed and wrapped his arm around her, pulling her close, so she could feel the heat of his body. "Considering our history here?"

"I definitely think so." He leaned over and gave her a kiss on the nose. "Now, figure out what you want to order."

The waiter came by to bring them water and bread, and Todd picked out a bottle of wine for them to share, Allison's favorite Pinot Noir from Willamette Valley in Oregon. She was delighted. Usually, they picked something different. Todd preferred heavy cabernets, so they would compromise, ordering something in the middle of their preferences or getting their own glasses. Resting her hand on his thigh, she gently stroked her way up his leg to his crotch, grinning to herself as she found him hard as she continued to pretend to peruse the menu.

"Do you know what you'd like?" His mouth was right next to her ear, so close, she could feel his lips moving against the sensitive curve. Giving up the teasing, she placed her hand directly on his crotch as she turned slightly.

"I'd like the steak, medium."

As she stroked his cock through his pants, his arm tightened around her, sliding down her upper arm to brush against her breast.

"Anything for an appetizer?" he asked.

"You choose whatever you'd like, I know what I want."

Before he could reply, Allison slid down, ignoring his startled exclamation as she swiftly positioned herself beneath the table.

"Princess," she heard him say, although his voice was slightly muffled. Allison ignored his warning as she swiftly unzipped him, releasing his dick from the confines of his pants. His fingers gripped the table on either side of her head, but she knew the tablecloth shielded her from being seen by anyone. Tugging at his hips, she pulled him closer, making him slump in the seat a little as she flicked her tongue, licking the drop of pre-cum from its tip. There was a small moan above her head.

It was like her own little secret cave of pleasure beneath the table. She wrapped her hand firmly around the base of his cock and opened her mouth, clamping her lips tightly around his shaft just underneath the head. As his sensitive head was pleasured by her tongue, the tip of it invading his pee-slit, Todd shuddered and gripped her hair for a moment.

Just as quickly, his hand was gone, and she could hear him talking to the waiter who had apparently returned with their wine. As Allison heard him presenting it to Todd, she slowly moved her head down the shaft, fitting just a little more of it into her mouth. Carefully bobbing her head to avoid hitting it on the table, taking him a little deeper with each stroke, the rest of the restaurant, and even the waiter conversing with her boyfriend, was completely unaware of her activities.

"It's very good," Todd said, his voice only slightly muffled by their positions. "Thank you."

Hearing the distinctive sound of liquid being poured into a glass, Allison tilted her head to take more of Todd's cock, pressing it toward the back of her throat, determined to fit the whole of it into her mouth. If she managed to do so while he was talking to the waiter, even better.

"Would you like to wait for the lady to order?"

With a low hum of pleasure, Allison sucked and pushed forward, taking his entire length until her lips were pressed to the base of his groin. She could feel Todd lean forward, doing his bit to keep her from view. She chuckled around his thick meat, sending all sorts of interesting vibrations through him.

"No, I know what she wants."

Well, that was an understatement. She could feel his dick pulsing against her tongue in happy pleasure. Pulling herself back as slowly as she could, she tried to breathe and suck quietly as Todd ordered their dinners. She could feel his thigh muscles clenching, his voice occasionally a little strained as she worked for her own special appetizer.

Almost as soon as she heard the footsteps of the waiter walking away, Todd's hands were beneath the table, pressing on the back of her head, fingers curving just under the largest collection of curls, pushing her down. Sucking even harder, her fingers kneaded his thighs, massaging them as he tensed. Another low groan was all the warning she had, then he was cumming, and she was frantically swallowing. Salty sweetness filled her mouth, sliding down the back of her throat and into her belly.

"Mmmm," she hummed as he filled her, the tension in his fingers and thighs slowly relaxing as he finished pumping his load between her suckling lips. Letting his dick slowly soften in her mouth, she finally allowed it to pop out, then gave it a kiss before peeking out from under the tablecloth. He was trying to look at her sternly, but the sides of his mouth were turned up.

"Is it safe?" she whispered. Black hair swayed as he nodded, a finger scooping a bit of cum off of her chin and pressing it to her lips. Licking it lasciviously, she pulled herself up next to him, just as the waiter came around the corner of the booth with their salads. Innocently she blinked at him as he looked at her in confusion. The bathroom was on the other side of the restaurant, and he was obviously trying to figure out how she'd gotten to and from it without him seeing her.

He set the salads down and left the table, a thoughtful look on his face, which had both of them laughing once he was out of earshot. Instead of talking about what was currently going on in their lives, being back in this restaurant had them reminiscing about their relationship. The beginning was rather sordid, but Allison found a lot of enjoyment in comparing notes with Todd. He even told her he hadn't been nearly as sure of himself as he'd seemed.

"I wasn't sure how I would ever face you again if you didn't show up at the library," he confessed. "It was one thing to hear you talk about what you wanted and know you enjoyed one night of losing control with me, but I wasn't sure if you or the cops would show up to meet me at the library to get the tape."

Allison laughed. "I wanted it too much. And by it, I mean what you were offering, not the tape, although that, too."

"Thank, God," he said fervently, and they both laughed. Allison snuggled closer to him, ignoring the spear of asparagus on her fork in favor of a kiss. Although she could possibly ascribe the warm fuzzy feelings inside of her to the wine, she knew it was this man, this crazy, wonderful, wild man, who had risked a lot to bring her fantasies to life, not knowing if she'd actually go through with indulging in them. It hadn't occurred to her at the beginning how much he'd been risking for her. Now, realizing how vulnerable he'd made himself in so many ways, not to mention how cute it was to hear him confess his early insecurities before she showed him exactly how much she wanted what he was offering, only made her love him more.

By the time the waiter came to clear their dinner away, Allison and Todd were about as wrapped around each other as a couple can be while sitting in a secluded restaurant booth. Under the table, she even had one of her legs hooked over and around his, her hand resting on his thigh. All the server could see was her head resting on his shoulder and his arm tucked around her waist, hand curved over her hip. Giving them a little smile, the server whisked away their plates, and Allison frowned.

"He didn't ask if we wanted dessert."

"He didn't need to."

She turned her head to peer suspiciously up at him. "The innocent look doesn't suit you. What did you order while I was in the bathroom?"

"It's a surprise," Todd murmured, his arm shifting to pull her closer and up toward him as his mouth slanted down on top of hers. She willingly parted her lips with a little moan, clinging to him. If they weren't in a restaurant, she'd probably be pulling him on top of her. Actually, that didn't sound like a bad idea… If they could keep the server away for long enough to take advantage of the fact they were seated in a booth...

Pulling his lips away, Todd pushed open her dress. The design gave him a shocking amount of access, his hands squeezing her breasts as he began to suckle at her nipple through the lacy bra.

"Oh, fuck..." she said softly, clutching at his head as he tormented the sensitive bud with his mouth. With every suck of his lips, her body seemed to pulse in answer. At the same time, she couldn't help but glance at the corner the server would walk around to the front of their booth—he could walk around it at any moment and see her scantily clad breasts, covered only by lace and Todd's hands and mouth. Fuck, that was hot. Teeth closed around one nipple, fingers plucking insistently at the other, Allison's head fell back as she gave a small whimper of pleasure.

Then he was sliding away, just as she had earlier, underneath the table—which considering how much bigger he was, was extremely impressive. Somehow, he slipped his broad shoulders down, almost pulling the tablecloth with him, but their combined efforts kept it from moving too much.

Now Allison was the one sitting in the booth, feeling rather exposed and very vulnerable, knowing someone could walk by at any given moment. Being under the table had felt much safer. Quickly, she pulled the sides of her dress up and over her breasts, still feeling exposed as Todd's hands slid up and down her bare legs. She preferred bare legs when it was warm enough, and now, she was extremely thankful for that. The faux wrap-around construction of her skirt made it easy for him to part it on either side of her legs, making her basically naked from the waist down, other than her lacy panties. She wriggled a little as she felt him ease them off, lifting her bottom so he could pull them down and away.

Hands pushed at the inside of her thighs, and she obediently spread them, her body quivering at the slightest sounds coming from the dining room, sure at any moment, someone was going to walk around the corner and know exactly what was happening in their secluded booth. Of course, that element of danger was half of the thrill and only made her more excited. Beneath her dress, her nipples were rock hard and rubbing against the lacy confines of her bra as she tried to control her breathing. Little kisses made their way up her inner thighs as Todd's hands slid under her buttocks and pulled her forward, bringing her to his mouth.

She had to stifle a moan as she felt his hot breath, followed quickly by his tongue on the open folds of her pussy. Sitting here in this booth, knowing at any moment, their server could return with their dessert, while Todd feasted upon her pussy beneath the table, was more than just a little exciting. Before Todd, she hadn't known how much a hint of exhibitionism and danger could get her off, but it was one of those things that just flat out did it for her. The color was high in her cheeks as she clutched at the table, trying to tilt her hips to offer him even more access without noticeably slumping in her seat.

One long finger pushed inside, sliding easily into her molten hole, and she shuddered, her body clenching around it. Todd's tongue licked all around her swollen folds as he began to fuck her with his finger, teasing her with slow, gentle strokes that made her want to beg him to touch her more, harder, faster. Of course, she couldn't because someone might hear, and she was already struggling to keep a normal countenance in case the server returned. How on earth had Todd handled ordering their meals while he'd been in this position?

A second finger slid in beside the first, curving in the most delicious way. Allison's eyes fluttered shut for just a moment, and she writhed, barely catching her low moan of pleasure. She managed to get herself under control just as the server came around the corner, setting down two spoons on their table.

"Would you like anything else?" he asked, eying the empty place next to her. "An after-dinner drink or coffee?" Either he was a really good actor, or he truly believed Todd was in the bathroom. Of course, Todd chose that moment to suck her clit into his mouth, and Allison bucked a little. She couldn't stop herself or the blush that rose in her cheeks as the server's expression turned to one of speculation. The fingers inside of her pumped wickedly, and she clenched in pleasure and as an automatic reaction to hold Todd's fingers inside of her, so she could focus.

"N-no, thank you," she managed to say. "I think we're fine."

The server gave her a long look, just the hint of a smirk on his face, and Allison did her best to keep her own expression bland, even though her cheeks felt like they were on fire, she was blushing so hard.

Almost as if he knew, having the server standing there, talking to her, was turning her on even more, Todd thrust his fingers hard and deep. Allison struggled to keep her body from arching as he sucked hard on her clit, her own fingers clutching at the edge of the table as she looked straight at the server and began to orgasm. The shock and delight on his face, the struggle to remain quiet, only spurred her to greater heights of pleasure as she rippled with ecstasy. One low moan escaped her as her clit throbbed in Todd's mouth, his tongue flicking against the sensitive nub, his fingers rubbing over her g-spot as her inner walls spasmed around him.

Her eyelids fluttered shut again for a moment, knowing the server was still standing there, watching her orgasm while Todd pleasured her beneath the table... She was completely out of control, and her body loved it. As she drifted down from the height of her climax, her eyes opened again to see the server smiling smugly, the front of his pants straining. Strangely, she no longer felt like blushing. She felt too good to be embarrassed, and he certainly didn't seem embarrassed.

"Dessert will be right out," he said before walking away.

Allison made a little face. How unfair. She orgasmed in front of him, but Todd wasn't going to have to go through the embarrassment of coming out from under the table in front of him? Her body relaxed as Todd's fingers withdrew, and the tablecloth shifted, her grinning boyfriend sliding onto the booth next to her. The smugness on his face matched the servers. She just smiled blissfully.

"Did you enjoy that?" he asked, leaning forward to kiss her, so she could taste herself on his lips, musky and bittersweet with a hint of honey. Their tongues dueled as she drank in his kiss.

"Yes," she said finally. "You know he saw me cum."

"I know you like an audience," Todd countered, his lips traveling down her neck, his hands caressing her hip. Her own hand had found its way back to his lap, where he was rock hard yet again. "And I know he didn't see anything I would be unhappy about." Well, she couldn't really argue with that. "Don't worry, we're not going to get kicked out of the restaurant."

"Oh, good, since I haven't had dessert yet."

Chuckling, Todd nipped the side of her neck before pulling away and rearranging them just before the server whisked around the corner, looking extremely smug. There even seemed to be an extra little bounce in his step before he put down a plate with a flourish.

For a few moments, Allison just stared, trying desperately to wrap her mind around the strangeness of the display. Truffles, a plateful of chocolate truffles in three concentric circles around a small pedestal, upon which sat a jewelry box—a small one.

"Todd..." she breathed, sucking air in through her lungs. The rest of the world seemed to melt away to nothingness as the server stepped back and disappeared, the hum of the restaurant fading as she tried to get over the sensation of being punched in the stomach.

"Allison," he said back, his deep voice serious. Cupping his hand under her chin, he turned her face toward him, and she blinked back tears, she hadn't even known were there until she was trying to look at him through them. His dark eyes were filled with warmth, a true depth of caring, and all the love she could have ever wished for.

"I lusted after you when you wouldn't even talk to me. I chased you down and fulfilled your fantasies, hoping it wouldn't get me arrested. I left you, so I could make myself into the man I wanted to be for you and prayed you would still want me when I returned. I never want to have to leave you again. I want to spend the rest of my life, lusting after you, talking with you, fulfilling our fantasies, and loving you with every ounce of my being. Will you—"

She threw herself at him, cutting him off as the tears ran down her cheeks, and pressed her lips against his, half-sobbing from sheer joy. There was no woman in the world luckier. They had started with his lust and her desperation and traveled a road together that had taken her so far beyond anything she'd ever thought to experience. That it had led her here, to this ecstasy of emotion, this joy... she was going to hold this man tight and never let him go.

"Yes... yes, yes, yes, yes," she chanted as she pulled herself away. "I love you."

"I love you, t—"

Laughter rippled through his body as she pressed herself against him again, smothering him with another kiss. They clung to each other, letting their bodies express the tide of emotions that surged through them, the things too strong, too hard to describe with mere words. Slowly their kiss gentled, their lips caressing each other. Todd finally pulled away, but only by a couple of inches, his hands still wrapped around her back.

"Can I show you the ring now?"

"Yes." Allison beamed at him.

Almost reluctantly, he pulled one arm away from her to snatch the box from the plate. Allison wriggled around, so her right side was leaning into him as he popped the box open.

"It's beautiful..." The main stone was about one carat in a brilliant-cut, with three tiny stones arrayed on either side for a total of six smaller stones. The band itself looked vintage, with lots of twists and curls, almost a tiny architectural framework connecting the bottom of the band to the top, the elaborate lattice of white gold curling around the stones. "I love it. It's perfect." She turned her head up and kissed him again.

Truthfully, she would have been happy with just about anything he wanted to give her and wouldn't have complained if it had been butt ugly, but she truly loved this ring. She loved the old-fashioned look, the intricate band, the fact the stone was noticeable but not overpowering. Todd wrapped his arms around her and slid it onto her finger, and Allison found herself blinking back more tears. The ring fit perfectly, the silver color bright against her skin.

"Now," Todd said into her ear, supporting her left hand with his, so they could both admire the ring on her finger. "I got the truffles so we could easily choose to stay here or go home."

"Home," she said in a husky voice. There was no way dessert could possibly hold her interest now. "Take me home."

6

The entire ride home, Allison couldn't stop looking at her ring. Not because it was beautiful, although it was, or because she was easily distracted by anything sparkly, although she was, but because of what it represented. Todd would never leave her again. The giddy feeling she got every time she looked at the ring was like an adrenaline rush.

"I'm glad you like the ring so much," Todd said, grinning as he caught her looking at it again. "Although I hope you don't forget to pay attention to me, too."

She laughed. "It's going to take some getting used to," she said. "It's so sparkly and distracting after all."

"Am I going to have to tie your hands down to keep from looking at it tonight?" The amused tone of his voice said he didn't really mind, after all, he kept looking at it as well. It was a very public marker, she belonged to him, and he liked the way it felt to see it on her finger, to know that she'd agreed to be his.

"I'd be okay with that," she purred, snuggling against him. Deliberately, she turned her hand to the side, so she couldn't see the course of her distraction anymore as she nuzzled his shoulder with her face.

"Did you know I was going to propose?" he asked, sounding almost like a little boy. There was a strange hint of vulnerability about him. "Or was it a total surprise?"

"Mostly a total surprise. I did notice you seemed extra... mmm... lovey lately, but nothing happened, so I thought maybe I was imagining it, or it didn't mean anything."

"When did you notice?"

"A couple of weeks after the housewarming party, then the past few weeks, you got all extra lovey again."

"Ah... A couple of weeks after the house warming party was when I started planning how I was going to do it. I bought the ring a couple of weeks ago," he said a little smugly.

"Well, I had no idea it was going to be tonight, or you were going to do it at all," she said, smiling dreamily at him. "I did *hope...*"

The smug look on his face was adorable.

Anyone watching them try to walk up to the house would have been highly amused by the rushing, slowing pace as they did their best to get to the house as quickly as possible, but kept getting distracted by wandering hands and hungry kisses. Finally, Todd picked her up in his arms, one arm cradled behind her back, the other beneath her knees, and carried her the rest of the way as Allison laughed and did her best to keep her skirt from falling open. Flashing the neighborhood was a little too far, even for her exhibitionist side—especially since Todd had yet to return her underwear.

She knew he was strong but was still impressed when he carried her all the way up to the bedroom. Once they were in the house, she'd given up the fight to keep her legs and bottom covered, wrapping her arms around his neck, peppering his neck and jaw with kisses. Todd pushed through their bedroom door, finally lowering his mouth to hers as he let her legs drop. Wobbly, Allison leaned against him as they stripped each other almost frantically, the pathway to the bed littered with their clothing.

Tumbling onto the bed, Allison laughed and pushed him down, so she was on top. Rarely did Todd let her take control, but right now, he didn't seem to mind. Hands digging into her hair, he pulled the pins out as she straddled his body. His eyes were glowing as she pressed down on top of him, the long length of his dick digging into her slit. Moving her hips back and forth, she rubbed her juices all over the underside of his cock, watching as his pupils dilated, his hands clenching in her curls. He pulled her down for a searing kiss, demonstrating, even though he was beneath her, he could still take control anytime he wanted.

Leaning into the kiss, Allison lined up the head of his large erection with her pussy, pressing down so just the tip nudged into her as their tongues swirled together. They moaned into each other's mouths as he breached the entrance to her body. Moving her hips in a circular motion, she stirred the inner lips of her pussy with his hard-on, pressing down to occasionally take the very tip of him into her body. She teased and tantalized them both as one of Todd's hands drifted down from her hair to begin massaging her breast, igniting her passion.

Rocking back, she took a little more of his cock, taking the entire helmet into her pussy. Lifting his hips, Todd tried to push into her tight sheathe, but she rose with him, denying him farther entrance than she'd already given him. Breaking the kiss, Todd pulled her partially upright with the hand gripping her hair, making her arch her back as his hand tightened on her breast.

"You'd better figure out what you're doing," he growled, his fingertips pinching her swollen nipple and making her gasp with delight.

"I just want to pleasure you," she said, lowering her head to his chest. He allowed the movement, though he didn't loosen his grip on her hair, and to be completely honest, she didn't want him to—it made her feel wonderfully submissive. "Please let me pleasure you." Another sharp pinch to her nipple had her writhing.

"Then pleasure me, Princess," his voice was low, filled with dark erotic promise. "But don't take too long."

The threat made her moan as she sucked his nipple hard into her mouth, nibbling on the small bud. He lifted his hips again, and this time, when she didn't impale herself, he didn't chastise her. Taking that as permission, Allison began to tease his nipples, rubbing her pussy all over the tip of his dick. It was exquisite torture, straining their nerves. His dick felt as if it would explode at any moment if he didn't get it inside her, yet he wanted to indulge her and was curious what she would do next.

After a few more torturous minutes, lavishing oral attention on his nipples, Allison sat back, her breasts bobbing slightly on her chest as she pressed down. They gasped with need and pleasure as the first few inches of his dick slid into her. Clenching her pussy, she enjoyed the feeling of him stretching out her tight hole. Still clenching hard, she pulled up and off again, teasing the tip of his dick with her wetness. Todd groaned, letting go of her hair, so she could do what she wanted—for now. Filling his hands with her luscious breasts, he squeezed them encouragingly as she moved on top of him. The snug tightness partially encasing his shaft was driving him crazy, and his balls ached with the need to bury himself in her wet tunnel.

She lowered herself again, just a few inches, maybe half an inch more than she had the first time. With a groan, he lifted his hips again, trying to shove into her, but she kept the same distance away. Gritting his teeth, he arched his back, his fingers finding her sensitive nipples, pinching them. Allison cried out as the delicious bite shot through her, from her turgid nipples straight to her pussy, as though he was transmitting his sexual frustration from his body to hers.

One last time, she lifted herself off of his dick, panting and crying out as he tugged on her nipples, not ordering her to come back down on him, but doing his best to give her ample motivation to lower herself. Allowing him to torture her breasts, shuddering with pain and delight, Allison hovered over him for a moment, suspended over his dick with just the tip inside her. She slammed down, crying out as he filled her completely, his length buried snugly in her pussy. Todd gasped, and his hips lifted of their own accord, pressing him even deeper into her body, and he had to concentrate on not immediately filling her with cum. With his hands on her breasts, he held her in place, trying to ignore her wriggling as her cunt grasped him like a vise and massaged.

Once he was under control, he released his death grip on her breasts, and she slumped on top of him. Half-hooded hazel eyes smiled down at him, enjoying the sense of power she was experiencing, loving how he quivered beneath her thighs, knowing he was on the edge of his control. She began to ride him with long slow strokes, lifting all the way to his tip before sinking back down again. It was a constant tug of war for him between his desire to cum in the intense, tight wetness of her pussy and the desire to have her bouncing on top of him for a little longer.

Although he yearned to change positions—to roll over, turn her onto her back, and spear her, satiating his lust in her while she cried out beneath him—he found he enjoyed giving her this semblance of power. He loved the way she looked, moving and arching, her hands splayed against his chest, her breasts bouncing in time with her ride. Biting his lip, he stifled a moan as he ran his hands up and down her sides. Allison could see just how much this slow lovemaking was teasing him. Her own pussy was burning with the need to take him harder and faster but was enjoying being in control too much to rush it.

Circling her hips, she lowered herself onto him and pulled herself up, using his dick to stir her insides as she did so. His body jerked at this strange new sensation. When she pressed against him, her circular motions ground her swollen clit and pussy lips against his groin, driving him wild. With a cry, he grasped her narrow waist, taking hold of her hourglass shape, trying to control her movements. Allison struggled a little, shushing him, and doing her best to continue her slow seduction, near torture for both. He was sure if he stopped concentrating, even for a moment, he would cum. The delicious sensations spreading through his body demanded release, and the only thing keeping him from cumming as she slowly fucked him was his own willpower.

Finally, Allison couldn't stand it any longer and began to rock harder, slamming her body up and down on him as he heaved and moaned beneath her. After three brutal thrusts, she ground her body down on his, her hips making those same circular motions, rubbing back and forth with her back arched. When he grasped her breasts, she thrust the soft mounds into his palms. Her nipples jutted out between her fingers as Todd's hands closed around the sensitive globes, his dick finally spewing forth frothy cum as he lost control.

The feel of him jerking inside her, knowing she had pushed him past his own limits, had Allison gasping with ecstasy as she rubbed her clit hard against his pubic bone. Feeling her own climax rising, she reached behind her to wrap her fingers around his balls. He was still gasping and moving, although he must have already been drained of his load of cum. She wanted to see if she could draw this out even more.

Kneading his balls gently, she tugged them away from his body. Her own body was starting to tighten as Todd thrashed beneath her and let out a primal cry as his sensitive cock hit overload. He was drained of his cum, yet the orgasmic feelings sweeping through his body continued at an incredible rate. Allison's pussy ground on top of him, the narrow passage gripping and clutching his mostly-hard dick as he spasmed inside of her.

Somehow, he had the presence of mind to slide one hand down from her breast to where their bodies were joined, finding her clit and pinching and rubbing it between his fingers and rapture exploded outward from the sensitive nub. It was her turn to thrash as her pussy heated and shuddered with an overwhelming climax as he took back control. The slight rocking of his hips thrust his mostly-erect penis back and forth, rubbing against her g-spot as she came for him. The continuous movement on his cock was almost painful, but he didn't let up until Allison slumped on top of him, his body still jerking with occasional aftershocks of the pleasure she'd heaped on him.

Carefully, he removed his hand from between their bodies, cradling her as she whimpered and slid to the side, leaving a streak of wetness across his thigh. After a few moments of heavy panting from both of them, he opened his eyes and looked at her, where her head was resting in the crook of his arm.

"Don't expect to get to do that too often," he said in a hoarse voice. "Even if it was amazing."

"You liked it," Allison said smugly.

"I like this, too," he said dryly as he grasped her by the back of the neck and pushed her head down toward his crotch, letting her know she wasn't quite done yet. Allison submitted gracefully, despite the fact she was tired. She wanted to please Todd, to show him how much she loved him. Which is why she'd taken control away from him for once. She'd known it wouldn't last—he liked being in control too much and she wanted him there—but giving him a bit of a fight for it was fun and so was the aftermath. She had to admit, she loved the way he took control when she started acting bratty.

The taste of sex filled her mouth as she licked him cleaned of their juices, taking his flaccid cock between her lips and sucking gently. For a few moments, he jerked and twitched as she worked him, even her gentle ministrations almost too much for his sensitive member after the extended orgasm she'd given him. Once he was clean, he pulled her back up, kissing her lips gently and tucking her into the crook of his arm before rolling onto his side and wrapping his other arm and one of his legs around her.

Happily, Allison snuggled into him, rubbing her face against the bristly hair on his chest.

This is how I'll sleep for the rest of my life.

It was where she belonged.

Unfortunately, it took less than two minutes the next morning for everything to go rapidly downhill.

Allison awoke refreshed. She stretched and felt a strange heaviness on her finger. Putting her hand out in front of her, she admired her ring. What a delightfully odd feeling to have that finger encircled. It really did make her hand feel heavier. The morning sunlight made it glitter as she thrust her hand into one of the spots where the sun was coming in through the curtains.

"Silly woman," Todd growled, right before his arm looped around her body and pulled her back down to the bed. Giggling,

Allison turned to look at him, but his eyes were still closed as if he was asleep. He looked adorably tussled with his dark hair flopping all over the place, quite happy to stay right where he was. So, she poked him. With a grumble, he half-opened one eye to glare at her. "What?"

"Get up."

"Why?"

"I want to call people and tell them," she said, wriggling away from his heavy arm. "Diana's going to kill me for not calling her *last* night as it is. The only way I can possibly make it up to her is calling her first thing this morning." Todd groaned and rolled onto his back as Allison hopped up and pulled on her favorite robe, the sexy red cotton one, neatly covering everything with a very thin layer of cloth. A thought occurred to her that dimmed her glee, but only a little. "I wonder if I should call my parents."

Part of her rejoiced in the idea she finally had a reason to reach out to them, one that forwarded her own agenda, but another part of her was fearful of their reaction. What if they rejected her again? Did she really want to call them when by all rights, they should have contacted her by now? Graduation was less than a month away, and she still hadn't heard from them.

"No need to," Todd replied as he lifted his arm to cover a yawn, doing his own early morning stretch. Although ten a.m. wasn't exactly truly early morning anymore, they'd had quite a night. "They're expecting us for dinner tonight."

She had just located Diana's number in her phone, but her finger froze above the little green icon that would initiate the call.

"Excuse me?"

With a smugly proud look on his face, Todd slid his hands behind his head, relaxing back on the bed. "They're expecting us for dinner tonight. Once I met your father and explained where I'm working and what my goals for my career are, he was happy to give his blessing for me to ask you to marry me."

It felt as though her ears were ringing. Something cold and hard settled in the pit of her stomach, weighing her down and simultaneously making her feel like other things might come hurling up.

Closing her eyes, Allison stood with her fists clenched, trying to get a hold on herself.

"Allison?"

The absolute fury in her eyes when she opened them turned them almost golden. Heat rose in her cheeks as she stared at her newly-minted fiancé, who was starting to look a little wary. Good! He should!

"You went and talked to my parents?" she asked quietly.

"Your dad, yes. A couple days ago," Todd said, giving a small sigh of exasperation. "This rift between you has gone on for too long, and it's completely unnecessary. The whole reason I went away last year was so I could put myself in a position where your parents would approve of me."

"That's not the point!" Allison snapped. Hurtling into movement, she opened her drawer and pulled out her underwear. If it was possible to put underwear on angrily, she personified the maneuver. "I don't care if they approve of you!"

"Well, I care," Todd snapped back. "How would you like it if my mom didn't approve of you?"

"It's not the same." She tugged a shirt over her head so hard, she almost ripped it. "She wouldn't cut you off from her life just because she didn't approve. My parents care more about giving their approval than they care about whether or not I'm happy. How am I supposed to know if they really love me if they're only talking to me again because I'm with a man they approve of?"

"Of course, they love you!" Todd threw his hands in the air as he got up from the bed, gloriously naked and angry. For once, she found herself less than appreciative of the view, mostly because she had no desire to be distracted from her justifiable fury.

"Well, they don't act like it!" Tears sparked in her eyes as the rejection and hurt she'd managed to keep clamped down deep inside surged, and she angrily turned her head away as she pulled on her jeans. "The whole point of not talking to them was I wanted to know they loved me enough to accept my decisions, to let me live my life by my choices because that's what made me happy. Now, you've gone and undermined *all* of that." To both of their horror, tears started to spill down her cheeks. Todd looked stricken as he moved toward her, holding out his hands pleadingly.

Deep down, she realized, given the chance, she probably would have called her parents. If not today, then probably sometime this weekend. But that didn't excuse completely taking the choice away from her.

"Allison, Princess, please... it's not a bad thing, they know the truth. Someone had to speak up first, and I thought it would be easiest for everyone if it was me. They love you, they just didn't know how to approach you, and I didn't mind approaching them."

"Well, learning might have been good for them!" She slapped his hands away and headed for the door.

"Where are you going?" Todd's voice got a little higher, a measure of his desperation to fix things. "Allison, I did this to make things right, for all of us, not to make them worse!"

"Too bad. I'm going to Diana's." Allison whirled around when she heard him moving toward her again, glaring at him through her tears. "Don't follow me." Turning back around, she hurried out the door in a whirl of self-righteous anger and betrayal.

Todd vented his own feelings by kicking the dresser.

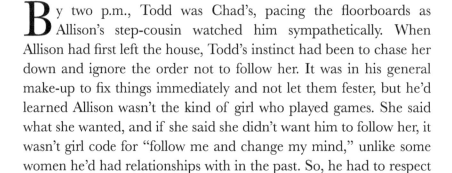

By two p.m., Todd was Chad's, pacing the floorboards as Allison's step-cousin watched him sympathetically. When Allison had first left the house, Todd's instinct had been to chase her down and ignore the order not to follow her. It was in his general make-up to fix things immediately and not let them fester, but he'd learned Allison wasn't the kind of girl who played games. She said what she wanted, and if she said she didn't want him to follow her, it wasn't girl code for "follow me and change my mind," unlike some women he'd had relationships with in the past. So, he had to respect that right now she wanted space—even if it was driving him up the wall.

"That entire side of the family is crazy, you know. I still can't understand why my dad married into it." Chad shook his head with a dramatic sigh. "Just give her time to calm down. She's much more reasonable when she calms down."

"And do you think talking to Diana will calm her down or just rile her up even more?" Todd asked with a sardonic look, which made Chad hesitate. While he didn't hold anything against Diana after their run of dating ended, he knew the little Asian was a bit of a spit-fire, and Todd wasn't always her favorite person. On the other hand, if Allison wouldn't be swayed by her parents, why would she be swayed by her friend? Todd paced, rubbing his hand through his hair over and over again in his agitation.

"It's as if she wants them to *prove* they love her enough to do what she wants. And they're on the other side, waiting for her to prove she loves them enough to do what they want."

"I'm a little more sympathetic to Allison's side on that," admitted Chad.

"Well, of course. Her parents were completely unreasonable, but they don't think they were. The best solution would seem to be, she chooses a guy she wants to be with, then he makes him into someone they would approve of." Stopping, he stood in front of Chad, throwing his arms out to either side in complete exasperation. "Hello, that would be me!" Growling, he tossed his hands up and resumed wearing a path in the floor of Chad's apartment.

Although they'd been frat brothers, he actually hadn't been particularly close to Chad until Allison. They'd gotten along okay, but it was her entrance into Todd's life that had really cinched their friendship. Especially since Allison had become much closer to Chad as a result. While Chad couldn't really be termed Todd's closest male friend, he was a friend Todd trusted and would have insight none of Todd's other friends would into the situation. Which is how he'd ended up over here after pacing his own house for three hours, waiting for Allison to come home. Other than replying to his query about whether she'd made it safely to Diana's, Allison hadn't responded to a single one of his text messages or picked up any of his calls.

Eventually, he hadn't been able to stand waiting around the house for her with no support of his own, so he'd called

Chad. Thankfully, the other man hadn't had any plans for the afternoon and been more than willing to be a sounding board. He liked
Allison and Todd, thought they were a great couple, and wanted
them to work things out. Even better would be if Allison could work
things out with her family because it would make the family dinners
and gatherings a lot less fraught with tension. For whatever reason,
his step-mother kept prodding delightedly at Allison's absence,
which made Allison's parents extremely defensive, and everyone
ended up miserable. He'd skip out on the dinners, but his father
begged him to be there, so he would have someone to talk to.
Bringing Allison back into the family fold, especially if she brought
Todd along with her, would make that aspect of Chad's life consid-
erably easier.

"The problem is, we're both right," Todd said, finally collapsing
on the couch with a sigh. His legs were tired from pacing, and his
energy seemed to have deserted him. The image of Allison's face,
hazel eyes large with betrayal, kept looming in his mind. That
wasn't how he'd wanted to make her feel. Yes, he'd known she'd be
upset about him talking to her parents, but he hadn't realized she'd
be quite *this* upset, or he never would have done it… probably…
maybe.

Okay, he wasn't sure if that was true. Part of his make-up was
he wanted to fix things. He'd seen how depressed Allison had been,
the past few weeks, although she didn't say it was because of her
parents. She talked a lot about graduation, and he'd quickly realized
how much it bothered her to think she might reach that major milestone, still estranged from her parents.

On top of that, he didn't want to marry Allison with this separa-
tion between her parents hanging over his head. He had worked too
hard and hated knowing how bereft she was about their estrange-
ment. That wasn't the way to start a new life together. Maybe he
should have waited, but he'd wanted to ask her to marry him when
they'd moved in together. Several months later, he'd realized she was
no closer to making up with her parents than she had been at that
point—further away, actually.

So, he had done what came naturally to him and decided to fix things to make Allison happy. It was pretty much his number one goal in life. Even if she wasn't particularly happy with him right now, he wasn't convinced he'd done the wrong thing.

"She'll forgive you," Chad reassured him, patting his shoulder and handing him a beer. "Eventually."

Todd grunted. *Eventually* being the operative word. If he needed any proof of how long Allison could hold a grudge, he only had to look at the detente between her and her family.

On the other hand, unlike her parents, he wasn't willing to let her shut him out—although she might not like his methods of making sure she didn't, he thought darkly.

7

———————

"It's a gorgeous ring," Diana said, studying it rather enviously. She and Allison were seated in the kitchen, while Roger was in the other room, taking up space on Diana's couch. He was pretending he was reading and not listening to their conversation—except for when he decided to put his own two cents in. Other than that, it was just like old times, back when she was living with Diana, and life was simpler.

Except it hadn't really been simpler. Back then, she'd still been torn between doing what her parents wanted and what she wanted, on top of the fact she'd been unhappily dating Roger and wishing Todd would come back into her life. Now that she had what she wanted, shouldn't she be happier?

She let out her breath on a puff of air, running her free hand through her hair. Diana had hold of her other hand and hadn't let go for the past ten minutes, studying the ring from every side, a wistful expression on her face.

So far, this visit hadn't gone quite as she'd expected.

First, she'd expected Diana to immediately agree with her about the perfidy of Todd's betrayal. She hadn't expected Diana to be more interested in hearing about last night's proposal rather than this morning's drama. Although from a feminine standpoint, it made a lot of sense, she wasn't used to Diana acting like... well, such a *girl*. Then had come the additional surprise that Roger was over and not inclined to leave, although he'd given them the courtesy of moving to the other room, so they could have a semblance of privacy.

Something was going on between him and Diana. She had a feeling Diana was being punished for something, much in the same way Todd occasionally punished Allison, which was unexpected from Roger—until she'd discovered, Todd and her ex had apparently become better buddies than she'd realized. Roger told her he supported Todd's actions and had, in fact, known about them beforehand and encouraged him to talk to her parents. Which had been the second big surprise of her visit.

The third came from the strange sense of deflation she had the longer she'd stayed. When she'd left the house this morning, she really hadn't wanted Todd to follow her. Now, back in her old apartment with Diana, she found she was already missing him, even if she was still mad, although that particular emotion was becoming harder to hold on to.

Still, there were some emotions being uncovered, now that they weren't masked by her anger—disappointment, hurt, betrayal, helpless vulnerability. And mixed into all of those, a strange sense of relief and love.

Now that she could think more calmly, she realized he'd done it *for* her. He hadn't meant to make her feel out of control, which is what the situation with her parents often made her feel, and going behind her back to talk to them had exacerbated that. Todd was used to being in control, not to mention protective, one of the things she loved about him—most of the time. It's not as if she could pretend she didn't know he was controlling.

He cared—enough to try to fix things for her, even if she hadn't wanted him to. It was a nice gesture, a loving gesture, just not one she appreciated at the moment.

"You aren't going to change your mind about marrying him, are you?" Diana asked, still holding Allison's hand in both of hers as she looked at her with worried eyes.

"No," she said definitively. That thought definitely hadn't crossed her mind. Okay, well, maybe it had crossed it, but she'd dismissed it immediately. Even the idea of taking the ring off caused her chest to constrict painfully. "I'm just so... so *angry*, and more than that. But at the same time, I know he meant well. It's just... it's *my* family. I should have been the one to make the decision whether or not to tell them about our engagement."

Diana pursed her lips thoughtfully. "What if the situation was reversed? Wouldn't you want things to have things settled between him and his mom before a major life-altering event? Especially if you'd been the inadvertent cause of the rift?"

Allison shift uncomfortably. She hadn't had much contact with Todd's mom other than a phone conversation here and there, but those had made her nervous at first because, of course, she'd wanted to make a good impression.

"Maybe, but I wouldn't have gone behind his back to do it," she retorted.

"Even if he was acting irrational about it and refused to discuss even the possibility of approaching her?" Roger asked in the driest voice she'd ever heard him use. Turning, Allison glared at the back of his head.

"There's no need for comments from the peanut gallery."

"Proving my point about your irrational viewpoint."

Deciding it was best to ignore Roger, she shrugged off his observation and pretended they didn't stick her, turning back to Diana.

"We could have discussed it together *after* we got engaged," she said, looking a little glumly at her ring. "There are certain things that should be joint decisions. I know I agreed to be submissive in the bedroom, and I tend to let him run things outside of it as well, but that doesn't mean he gets to completely run my life or make unilateral decisions completely opposed to what he knows I want, without even talking to me about it."

"That I agree with."

"Shut it," Diana snapped with a bit of her old spark as she glared at her boyfriend. Roger turned his handsome blonde head to give her an amused but quelling look, Allison recognized well. Although she'd never seen it on Roger's face, she'd seen it enough on Todd's. It promised later retribution for brattiness but in a most likely pleasurable manner. There was a little sparkle in Diana's brown eyes that said she knew it, too and didn't mind. Allison couldn't help but smile at her friend's happiness, thinking it both strange and wonderful, things had turned out the way they had.

"You're right... but Todd's right, too, which unfortunately means, nosy over there is also right." Roger coughed, and Diana ignored him. "You have been kind of unreasonable about your parents, and from an old-fashioned guy's perspective, he probably wanted to do the right thing and at least let your parents know before he proposed. He has a lot of pride, so it's probably bugged him you've kept him hidden from them. He probably wanted to clear up any misunderstandings and see if they would accept him before he asked you."

Allison made a face. "But I don't care whether or not they accept him."

"Doesn't mean he doesn't." Diana gave her a pointed look, and Allison sighed her acceptance. If the situations were reversed, she would definitely feel uncomfortable, Todd's mother didn't accept her. Not that she'd met her yet, but they'd talked on the phone several times, and the conversations had gone really well. "But you're also right about him taking the reins on an issue where he probably should have at least consulted you. Unfortunately, I don't really see a good compromise for the situation."

"Probably cause there really isn't one," Allison said ruefully. "We were at opposite ends of a spectrum, and there was no way to meet in the middle... not if he was going to surprise me." She sighed. "I guess this means I'll have to forgive him."

"You could make him work for it." Diana grinned wickedly. "It might be good for him to grovel."

"I wouldn't hope too much for that," interjected Roger. "Apologize, yes, grovel, no."

"Would you grovel?" Allison asked, actually looking for his opinion for the first time since she'd arrived at the apartment. Of course, she hadn't needed to ask him before because he had offered it freely.

Turning around, Roger slung his arm along the back of the couch and gave his girlfriend a dazzling grin.

"For Diana? Absolutely. But I'm a different kind of guy. For Todd, giving an apology *is* like groveling." He gave Allison a pointed look, one obviously meant to remind her there was a reason she'd dumped him and ended up with Todd. "And you should remember that."

She made a face at him, and he grinned again before turning back around and going back to pretending to ignore them. Diana squeezed her hand, regaining her attention.

"So, what are you going to do?" Diana asked.

That was the big question. After talking with Diana and Roger —and calming down a bit—Allison had to acknowledge Todd had some good reasons for his actions. On the other hand, she also had some good reasons for being mad. Yet, even though she was still upset, she was starting to wish she was talking to him, not her friends. Silly to miss him after only a few hours, but she'd gotten used to having him as her rock to lean on, and even though he was the cause of her current state, she wanted her usual rock.

"I guess I'm going to go home and talk it out with Todd."

Diana nodded, smiling. "I think that's a good idea."

"The hallmark of a good relationship is being able to handle adversity," said the peanut gallery. Allison couldn't help but roll her eyes and be glad Roger couldn't see her smiling. Although she definitely wasn't interested in him in any kind of way other than friendship, she had to admit he had become a lot more interesting since she broke up with him, and he started dating Diana. A change in character similar to the one she had gone through after meeting Todd, perhaps. He was definitely a lot more amusing, now he wasn't so focused on being polite and gallant all the time—a lot more annoying, too.

"Thanks for talking with me... both of you," she said, giving Diana a hug. She gave Roger a hug on her way out of the door. Some of what he'd said *had* helped her, even if she hadn't been looking for advice from him. Getting a guy's perspective had been nice, although she was annoyed with him for encouraging Todd to talk to her parents. At least it showed her Todd wasn't the only idiot male in the world, who thought it was a good idea.

~

When she got home, Todd wasn't there. She wandered around the house, looking for him, even going so far as to knock on the door to the playroom. The urge to go inside was more overwhelming than it had ever been before.

Was she subconsciously looking for some kind of punishment? Or maybe just some kind of release? There was no denying, sometimes their rougher sexual activities ended cathartic, and she'd had some pretty big emotional ups and downs over the past twenty-four hours, especially now. She was getting nervous about having walked out on him this morning rather than staying and listening to his side of things.

Granted, she'd been pretty angry, but now, she was feeling bad about her complete lack of communication.

Then again, part of what she was angry about was his lack of communication.

Except if he'd told her he wanted to talk to her parents before asking her to marry him, he wouldn't have been able to surprise her...

Gah.

There was just no way to avoid going around in circles, which is why she wanted him here. It only took her about twenty minutes of impatient waiting before she decided to text him.

Hey... I'm sorry I left so abruptly this morning. I'm home now, and I'd like to talk when you get home.

Jiggling her phone around in her hand, she decided to watch some TV to pass the time. Maybe calling him would have been a better idea since she would have gotten a response immediately, but if they'd started talking, she probably would have started the conversation about this morning and wanted to do that in person.

Talking out deep issues over the phone seemed like a poor substitute for face to face when they actually lived together. It would be one thing if they were a long-distance relationship, but as it was...

Yech. Even in her head, she was babbling. Being on the outs with Todd was extremely uncomfortable. Fortunately, he didn't make her wait long before texting back.

I'll be home soon.

She made a face at her phone before dropping it on the couch next to her. Soon... what defined soon? It could be anywhere from one minute to thirty, maybe more. Although Todd was pretty good about being on time for things, so hopefully, he wouldn't make her wait long. There really wasn't anything on television to garner her interest. Saturday afternoons were not exactly prime viewing hours. Ooooh... *Law and Order: SVU* marathon! She and Diana used to call it *Law and Order: FUS*, as in Fucked-Up Shit, which it was, but it was also a damn good show. Since she hadn't seen the current episode, she had a chance of being sucked in, so the time didn't go by so slowly.

Actually, she was so deeply involved in the mystery of finding out who killed the little girl, by the time Todd got home fifteen minutes later, she didn't run to meet him. Well, that was partly due to her own pride since she didn't want him to think he was immediately forgiven. It didn't take him long to find her, put his hands on her shoulders from behind, and lean down to kiss her left temple.

"FUS?"

"Well, I had to do something while I waited for you to get home," she said, a hint of banter in her voice to let him know she wasn't truly angry anymore. "And I hadn't seen this one."

"Ah," he said as he came around the side of the couch, sitting down and sliding his arm around her shoulders. "Hence the lack of interest in my return."

She made a little huffing sound, not quite an answer. She wasn't disinterested in the fact he was back... but now he was here, she still wasn't quite sure what she wanted to say to him… or him to her. And it really was a good show. Part of her wanted to stand her ground and make him 'pay' for going behind her back, but the truth was, she liked cuddling with him and wanted to snuggle into his warmth. So, she did, deciding pride wasn't worth giving up cuddling.

Todd curved his arm around her, tucking her in even closer, and rested his chin on top of her head. Whether or not she was angry at him, she liked being in that little nook. She appreciated he didn't want to get back into the argument, the second he got home.

"So, where'd you go?" she asked when the next commercial break came up.

"Chad's."

"Oh, yeah? What'd he have to say?" she asked curiously, moving away from him just enough, she could see his face. As she moved her upper body away, Todd reached out and grabbed her legs, pulling them over his lap, and Allison giggled as he raised one of his eyebrows at her. Even now, when they hadn't made up yet, he managed to make her feel loved and as if he couldn't get enough of her. Another girl might not allow him to maneuver her around, might try to make him work harder, but Allison didn't think he'd done anything out of malicious motivation, and she wasn't going to play games. She was ready to work things out and acted like it.

"He's missed you at the family dinners," Todd teased gently, rubbing his hand over her ankle as Allison bristled, eyeing him suspiciously. She was only ready to forgive if he was ready to ask. "He thinks your parents have been unreasonable and understands why you've been waiting for them to make the first move."

Looking into his dark brown eyes, Allison could see the warmth and understanding.

"I thought you understood that, too."

"I did… do." He ran his hand through his hair, ruffling it the way he did when he was searching for the right words. Hiding a little smile, Allison did her best to keep a stern look but knew her expression had softened. It always did when he ruffled his hair like that. "But I think it had also become pretty obvious, they are just as stubborn as you are, and someone needed to break the ice. I think they even realized they were wrong to try to make you do everything their way but are also worried about you and think they know the best way to make sure you're happy and secure."

"It would have been nice to hear it from them."

"None of you would have heard anything. I think you're all stubborn enough to sit around and wait for someone else to make the first move." Todd raised his eyebrow at her again, this time in a challenging way. "Would you have eventually decided to be the bigger person and reach out?"

"You still should have talked to me before talking to them," Allison said grumpily, although she couldn't argue his point. Maybe the stalemate with her parents had gotten a little ridiculous. Sure, they were unreasonable, but in a lot of ways, so was she. Was she really expecting her proud parents to come crawling to her? Talking to them, as long as she held her ground, wouldn't be considered crawling on her part, but she'd found it easier to keep pushing it off and concentrate on the other things in her life that were easy and made her happy.

Deep down, she knew her parents probably wouldn't have turned her away if she'd gone back to talk to them, even if she'd insisted on going her own way in life. The only thing that had been keeping her from doing so was the fear, maybe they did care more about their status than her and her own pride. The pride she got from them, the same pride probably keeping them from her. That was an unsettling thought, mostly because she didn't want to be as unrelentingly proud and uncompromising as her parents.

"Yes, I should have," Todd said, interrupting her thoughts as he reached out to cup her cheek, rubbing his thumb over her soft skin. Allison turned her head to press her lips against his palm. "But then the proposal wouldn't have been a surprise. Every time I brought up trying to talk to your parents, you became kinda unreasonable." A small smile played on his lips, and she smiled back reluctantly, knowing he was right.

"I just don't want you making unilateral decisions about things that affect both of us. Especially when it comes to something to do with my family."

"I won't… at least, I'll try not to. I definitely won't do it again on purpose." Reaching for her, he pulled her onto his lap, wrapping his arms around her waist as she placed her hands on his face, tipping his head back to look at her. "That wasn't my intention. But I don't think there's ever going to be anything else I would need to keep from you, anyway. I'm only planning on proposing once."

"Oh, well, that's good to know."

They smiled at each other.

"I just want to make things right for you. Always. I hated seeing how depressed you were whenever you talked about graduating. I could practically see you thinking about them and wondering if they were going to be around for that. Also, considering how many points I already had against me in their books, I figured asking for their blessing about proposing to you would probably give me a few points in my favor."

"Blessing, not permission?"

He gave a little growl. "Do you think I'm the kind of guy who asks for permission to marry my girlfriend? Besides which, you don't need your parents' permission for anything. You can make up your own mind. I just wanted them to know my plans, and they obviously thought they knew what your answer would be."

"Well, that's good," she said thoughtfully. She liked that Todd hadn't asked for permission, yet had still given a respectful nod to the old-fashioned custom.

"I just wanted to fix things for you. I couldn't stand seeing you unhappy when there was something I could do about it, and on top of that, I wanted your parents to know who I was and to know I was taking care of you."

"I do understand, I really do," she said with a sigh, running her hand over his chest. "And I accept you had the best of intentions."

"If it helps, I think your parents still aren't thrilled, you're with an up-and-coming businessman instead of someone who's already more established," Todd teased. "But because they miss you and love you, they grabbed at the chance to talk to me and have me help mend the breach."

"Actually, that does help a little," she teased, snuggling into him as the show came back on. They watched without talking until the next commercial break, which was also the end of the show. Allison sighed in contentment.

"I am sorry about storming out this morning," she said ruefully. "I needed the space to cool off, but I shouldn't have just left like that."

"It's alright." Todd shifted her around in his arms to a more comfortable position. "I understood. And I should have told you in a better way."

"I could maybe wish you were a little less understanding," Allison murmured, sliding her nails up the back of Todd's neck into his hair, raising goosebumps along his skin as he gave a small shiver.

"Oh, really?"

"Yes." She curled her fingers through the silky soft strands along the nape of his neck, giving him a coy look. "I'd really like to see what our sex room looks like, you know."

There was a moment of silence as Todd mused over her words, his cock hardening beneath her bottom. It wasn't the first time it had done that since she'd gotten on his lap, but it had a tendency to waver off and on since they hadn't been doing anything sexual.

"Alright," he said, slowly standing as he shifted her around in his arms, a wicked grin spreading across his face. Allison felt her body tighten in excitement. "I think I'm ready to show you."

As he flipped her over his shoulder, so she was hanging down with her face at the small of his back, she gave a small shriek and laughed as he moved toward the stairs.

"I can walk, you know!"

Todd slapped her upturned ass, eliciting another shriek.

"I prefer you like this."

The area he hit smarted, but in a good way. Allison grinned as she hung over his shoulder. Not only was she going to get to see the room, but she felt quite certain, she was heading for a very *pleasurable* punishment. Taking the lead last night had been a lot of fun, but right now, she couldn't think of anything better than being at Todd's mercy.

"I think I'm going to like being married to you."

8

The room was dark and erotically gorgeous.

Todd preceded her into the room after setting her down outside, so she could take off her clothes. She'd walked in to find him adjusting what looked like a gynecologist's exam table, only this one had leather restraints where no true doctor's table would.

What really caught her attention was the floor-to-ceiling to that completely covered the far side of the room. No matter where they were in the room, at least one of them would be able to watch their reflections in the mirror. Suddenly, she realized the apparatus she must have been bent over the last time was facing that mirror. Todd would have been able to watch every facial expression, every twitch of her body as he'd caned her, and if she hadn't been blindfolded, she would have as well.

The beauty of such an arrangement stunned her, and she had the immediate desire to watch Todd wreaking his erotic havoc on her restrained and willing body.

Aware Todd had turned his attention to her, Allison ignored him and looked around the room. Since he hadn't calling her over, she assumed he was willing to indulge her curiosity and wanted to take advantage of it while she could.

The floor was hardwood, and a few places had what looked like bolts and rings drilled into it. The spacing of the rings seemed significant—no need to guess what their use might be. There were more rings hanging from the ceiling, some near the rings on the floor, others over other apparatus. There was something that looked like a cross between a gymnastics horse and a balance beam, both well padded. The thing she had been bent over last time looked like a massage table, with select sections cut out and redesigned, tilted forward to put the subject's ass in the air. Across the room was a wooden beam, polished smooth, with a narrow, rounded top, just below hip height. Along the walls were various instruments of torture—flogs, crops, canes—and the wall right next to her had an armoire, she was sure held even more. A Saint Andrew's cross was set up near where a multitude of whips were hanging, so Todd wouldn't have to step far away if he wanted to change what he was using.

There was nothing resembling a bed.

"So, what do you think?" Todd asked, leaning against the gyno table, his arms crossed over his broad chest. He'd taken off his shirt but was still wearing his jeans. He looked mouth-wateringly good but extremely intimidating.

"I think…" Allison looked around the room again. "I think we could spend a lot of time in here."

A wide, anticipatory grin spread across his face. "I think so, too." He patted the table next to him, and his voice lowered to a purr. "Now, get your pretty little ass over here."

She was too excited to argue, wondering what he was going to do, what would happen next. The table was set up sideways to the mirror, so she could watch if she wanted, but it would be from the side. Keeping her focus on him would be much more intimate and erotic. She was a little disappointed the mirror wouldn't be very useful this time around, but there would be plenty of other times.

Todd helped her up onto the table and her feet into the stirrups, putting her arms over her head and restraining them, so she was stretched out and her ass was just at the end of the table. He wrapped another leather strap around her ribcage, just underneath her stomach, and one around each thigh and ankle, completely immobilizing her. Allison shuddered at the smooth embrace of the leather around her body and limbs, loving the security of being wrapped up by Todd. It was strangely comforting for something that made her so vulnerable. Spreading the stirrups, Todd pushed her legs far apart until her muscles began to strain.

"That's enough," she said, pleading. "It hurts…"

He had spread her so wide, her pussy lips were gaping open, and her knees slightly pointed up to give him the best possible view of her vulnerable assets.

"Alright, Princess," he murmured, his eyes flashing with something like amusement. She knew he wasn't actually laughing at her, just at the fact she was complaining about it hurting when she knew more erotic punishment and pain would soon be on the way.

Adjusting a few levers, he secured the stirrups in that position, then went to get a gag, silencing any more protests or pleas. Taking one of her hands, he put a bean bag in it, curling her fingers around the malleable object.

"If you need to safeword, just drop this."

Her pulse spiked, and her eyes got big, pupils dilating. Allison always trusted Todd not to push her past her limits, and they'd had plenty of time to explore what those limits were. She rarely needed something extra when she was gagged, trusting he would know when to stop. The fact he was giving her a way to end their play-time, despite her gag, added a depth of vulnerability and anxiety that set her heart racing—especially since this wasn't a real punishment. Then again, he never gagged her when he was actually punishing her.

It might just be a prop to tantalize her mind. If so, it was working.

Allison quivered in her bonds, anticipation high. The bean bag pressed against the underside of her engagement ring, a symbol of his possession, reminding her, she and Todd were going to be doing this for the rest of their lives. It added an entirely new level of intimacy to the proceedings, making her ache inside with overwhelming joy. She wanted him to do this to her—possess her, feed the needs burning inside, no one else had ever seen or bothered to discover.

There was something so freeing about having no control, willingly giving it over to him. She walked to the table, put herself on it, and allowed him to secure her, making the choice to let him take her to a place of pain and pleasure.

With rounded hazel eyes, she watched as he walked over to the wall, choosing a whip. He picked one with multiple strands, long and flexible, one she hadn't seen before. Each rubber strand was about a foot long and made a whistling sound as he swung it experimentally through the air. Stopping at the armoire, he opened it and pulled out nipple clamps and a bottle of something she couldn't quite see from one of the drawers before coming back to her.

"This is going to be… interesting," he said, a glint in eyes that made her shiver with anticipation a person gets when they're about to have their curiosity satisfied. Setting the implements of torture on a small table next to her, he brushed one brown curl off her face, admiring her hazel eyes with their flecks of gold, filled with trust and anticipation. She was so beautiful… and all his. Gently he leaned over, and her eyelids fluttered shut. He kissed each one, and she moaned in the back of her throat.

Going to stand between her splayed thighs, he ran his fingers up her pussy, smiling as she attempted to arch her back to meet his hands and found she couldn't, thanks to the straps across her body and thighs. Her eyes pleaded for a firmer touch. She was already completely soaked, the smell of her arousal slowly filling the air around them.

Lowering his lips to that wet mouth, he gently blew on her heated flesh, making her moan as he teased her body. Lasciviously, he licked along the insides of her thighs, letting his tongue linger as he got closer to her swollen flesh. Little muffled noises begged him to come closer to her core. Ignoring her body's pleas, he spread her ass cheeks with his fingers and slipped his tongue into that confined space, wriggling the tip against her tight anus, awakening the nerve endings clustered there. Allison groaned and tried to heave her hips to get her body to open farther, so he could really lick that small hole… to no avail.

Her pussy was leaking like a sieve from his teasing, her lower body on fire with sexual hunger. The air was cool against her hard nipples, which were standing proud and neglected on her chest, begging for attention as much as the rest of her.

Moving up from her ass crack, he lapped up all the juices he encountered until his tongue delved between the swollen folds of her pussy. Allison wriggled her hips as much as she could, trying to get the most contact out of this teasing encounter. With a mischievous grin, he started to write out "I L-O-V-E Y-O-U" with his tongue on her sensitive flesh. Of course, Allison was too heated to realize what he was doing, but it got a satisfying reaction as his tongue made seemingly random dips and swirls against her hot flesh. She was sinking into a sea of sensuality, burning with rampant desire, she had lost complete control over. If she hadn't been gagged, she would have been begging him to fuck her.

When Todd moved away from her pussy, she wanted to scream with frustration. She'd been on the brink of an orgasm. If he'd just tapped her clit she would have exploded, but nothing touched that sensitive nub except the air from the room, leaving her to writhe with passionate longing. Watching her struggling against the bonds, trying to find satisfaction for her aching pussy, Todd smiled and picked up the bottle.

He squirted some of the oil onto his hands, and the smell of cinnamon filled the air. Standing between her legs, he was careful not to stand close enough, she could rub herself against him—just close enough to tease her with the idea. Reaching up to her gorgeous breasts, the heaving globes accepted his touch eagerly, her encouraging moans begging for more attention to her sensitive appendages.

At first, she thought that the sensation of tingling heat was coming from the friction of his hands on her breasts and her dire need for stimulation, but it soon became apparent her skin was actually heating. Her nipples were turning into burning torches on her skin, itching with the need to be pinched, sucked, abused. Without realizing, she was writhing as she made pitiful mewling noises, her sensitive breasts tormented by the oils sparking her nerve endings.

Arching her back as much as she could, she wailed behind her gag as she realized there was no relief from the tingling fire he'd created. He was going to tease and torment her before allowing her to find any kind of fulfillment. Todd grinned evilly at her despairing expression and pinched her nipples hard. The rough touch gave her a kind of satisfaction, and she writhed like a cat in heat, the biting pinch helping to push back some of the feverish need riding her.

Allison let out a muffled cry when he trailed his fingers down to her pussy, squirted more oil onto his hands, and began to rub it onto her smooth mons and down into her sensitive folds. Allison's eyes closed against the glee on his face, her focus on the devastating sensations he was creating in her body as she spasmed in the throes of erotic need.

She screamed with frustrated passion as he inundated her cunt with the oil, her body jerking as he slid two fingers into her hole, creating a burning path straight into her needy core. Another finger pressed into her tight ass, and she almost dropped the bean bag— not because she wanted to end what was happening but because her entire body was now spasming, her fingers flexing as her inner muscles clenched, trying to find release. Her insides were as boiling hot as her outside, and she could feel the heady rush of a climax quickly approaching.

Gripping the bean bag hard to make sure it wouldn't fall, Allison gave herself over to the thrust of his fingers, her entire body tensing as the throbbing orgasm burst and engulfed her. Todd rubbed and stroked her inside, the passionate climax doing nothing to quench the heat of the oil. She sobbed as her flesh became even more sensitive in the aftermath of her orgasm. Everything felt twice as intense, the searing heat doubly punishing her sensitive nerves.

Todd stepped back for a moment and enjoyed watching her squirm, his dick rock hard as she pulled and struggled with her bonds and the burning passion. Her body was one big sexual itch, dying to be scratched, and she was helpless to do anything about it.

Carefully, he wiped his hands off on her thighs, making another part of her tingle.

With lust in his eyes, Todd picked up the nipple clamps lying off to the side. He pinched and pulled at her nipples with his free hand, his ministrations making the little buds burn even more, before replacing his fingertips with the clamps. Less than a minute later, her breasts were both adorned with silver, the biting pain of the clamps actually doing quite a bit to counteract the burning the oil had kindled. It was a different kind of pain, although it didn't make her any less horny as the pain fed her pleasure.

Tears of sexual frustration leaking from her eyes, her pussy was hot and ready for stimulation—*any* kind of stimulation.

Todd picked up the whip.

SMACK!

Allison screamed as the rubber bit into her open pussy, a thousand angry bees stinging her open and vulnerable flesh. It hurt more than any other whip he'd used on her, the flexible strands slapping hard, and the biting pain sliced through the heat of the oil. As she struggled and thrashed, Todd admired the way her pussy had puffed up in response to the whip—rubber would smart, but it wouldn't damage her. He liked the way her hips thrust upward, despite the pain, as if she was asking for more.

So, of course, he felt the need to oblige.

THWACK!

Another scream behind the gag muffled into a high-pitched moan.

SMACK! CRACK! THWAP!

Rhythmically, he beat her pussy, careful not to hit her too hard and giving her a moment between landing blows. Occasionally, he would snap the whip at her breasts, turning the creamy undersides a light pink, coloring part of her stomach when the whip landed.

With every slap against the inflamed folds of her cunt, her pussy responded with more fluid, growing wetter and puffier, throbbing with exquisite pain and burning with unrelieved pleasure.

CRACK! SMACK!

The engorged bud of her clit was growing larger, and Todd

amused himself, trying to land blows directly on it, giving Allison the sensation of buzzing pain, centered on her most sensitive organ. Her poor pussy gushed with fluid as she had a small orgasm, her cunt spasming emptily.

As she came down from the shuddering climax, she felt tired and weak, and the burning seemed to have lessened.

Todd stepped close again, putting the whip down. He stripped off his jeans, and Allison's heart jumped in the hope he was going to fuck her. Instead, he toyed with the clamps on her nipples, twisting them back and forth and tugging them, so the tender buds were stretched to their utmost limits. As she moaned and whimpered, he released her nipples from the tight confines of the clamps, then pinched and massaged them to encourage the renewal of blood circulation. Allison wailed as the pain spread through her, adrenaline pumping through her tired limbs and waking them.

Lowering his mouth, Todd sucked her sweet bud between his lips, simultaneously reaching a hand between her legs and sliding two fingers up and down the wet folds of her pussy before burying them in her hole. Almost against her will, tired as she was, Allison responded to the invasion, her hips lifting as much as possible, pressing her pussy against the palm of his hand. Alternating between nipples, sucking and biting them, he brought her sexual need back to a peak, her eyes sparkling with arousal as he masterfully manipulated her body's responses.

Beneath his hand, her pussy quivered with hunger, and her nipples popped in and out between his lips. When she began to heave beneath him, her body wriggling with renewed need, he knew it was time.

With one hard thrust, he buried himself, his hard groin slamming against the swollen, punished pussy folds. She yelped and thrashed as he fucked her, mercilessly riding her despite her abused pussy lips. His cock slid back and forth, stretching her ruthlessly, giving her no time to adjust as he dug his fingers into her hips and rutted with her with all the force of his own pent-up need.

The leftover oil in her pussy set his groin afire, and he groaned with the heat. The way she basked in his abuse of her body, her ecstatic clenching around his thrusting cock, left him no doubt she was his and always would be. As he fucked her, her hands twitched, and he saw glimpses of the ring on her finger, light glinting off the diamond every time he thrust into her. It only inflamed him more to see it on her hand, to know she had agreed to be his. His thrusts became harder, more demanding, guttural groans from the back of his throat rising as he invaded her bound body and felt her response.

Beneath this heady onslaught, Allison was thrilling to the sensation of having his cock moving inside her and the uncontrolled expression on his face as his rampant desire overtook him. With a cry, half-moan half-scream, Allison trembled as she reached the highest heights of her pleasure and tipped over. Her eyes fluttered, and a few tears leaked out as her body peaked, the ecstasy filling her up and overflowing, unable to come down from the pinnacle, forced to continue past the point of bearing by the pounding cock ravaging her body.

As Todd watched her face turn from ecstatic to agonized, as the force of her orgasm turned exquisitely painful, he could feel the rippling muscles of her pussy having their intended effect. Leaning forward, he used her hips as leverage to bury himself in her brutally hard, her muffled shrieks encouraging him as her breasts practically vibrated on her chest, jiggling so hard from the force and tempo of his thrusts.

Mine, mine, mine, mine... The word seemed to chant in his head with every spurt of his cum as he filled her, their sexual juices mingling as Allison shuddered through the last of her ring of orgasms. Todd collapsed on top of her, his head pillowed by her abused breasts as he groaned and finished pumping her with his seed.

She was too dazed to do anything but lie there as Todd finally stirred and released her from the restraints. As he massaged her limbs, making sure she didn't get any cramps, she gave him a sweet submissive smile, her eyes half-hooded with the lazy pleasure still humming through her.

Her legs were a little too wobbly to support her, and Todd was just as tired, but he lifted her into his arms and carried her across the hall to their bedroom, extremely thankful it wasn't far away from the sex room. Perhaps he should reconsider putting a bed in there… It would certainly make some things a lot easier.

They curled up together on their bed, Allison's body sore in all the right places. She felt much better than she had this morning, all the tension utterly drained out of her.

"Go to sleep…" Todd murmured into her hair, cradling her close in a protective and comforting way. "We'll nap. There's plenty of time before dinner with your parents tonight."

Caressing her gently, he stared down at her in wonder. It astounded him over and over how much trust Allison put in him. Of course, he made sure to give her ways to stop the action, like the bean bag, but he knew it was a point of pride with her to take everything he dished out. Knowing she literally handed him the keys to her body, again and again and was ready and more than willing to pledge to do so for the rest of her life was the most astounding thing. When he first met her, he'd never dreamed their relationship could go this far.

"Mmm-hmm." Nuzzling her face into his chest, she bit him lightly and felt him wince before his hand came down hard on her bottom. The bite had been because she still wasn't happy he hadn't talked to her beforehand, but she had to admit, she wasn't entirely against talking to them now.

The afternoon had done a wonderful job of relieving her stress and tension. The thought of dinner with them tonight didn't seem so bad after all. She drifted off on a wave of happy, cloudy, sleepy bliss.

9

Figuring out what to wear to her parents was almost as nerve-wracking as going on a first date. At first, she'd started to put on the kind of demure, elegant dress she always wore for dinners with her parents, a navy-blue conservative sheath. Then she'd stopped about halfway through and sat on the bed.

"What's wrong?" Todd asked, adjusting his tie.

She looked him over, from his dark, perfect hair to his concerned eyes, down his crisp white shirt to the dark grey slacks and his polished black shoes. There was a sports coat he was going to wear with it. The perfect image of the man her parents wanted her to end up with.

Meeting his eyes, Allison shook her head.

"We can't do this." Todd raised his eyebrows, his hands stilling their movements on his tie. She nodded at his attire. "*This.* The whole point was I want to live my own life and want them to accept who I've become. And right now..." Standing again, she let the dress fall to the floor. "We're not going to a formal dinner. We're not even going to one of their godawful family dinners. It's just us and them, right?" Todd nodded, and Allison headed back to the closet.

With a small, bemused smile on his face, Todd followed her.

To give her mother credit, her smile barely flickered when she took in what Allison and Todd were wearing. Todd had talked her out of going in the jeans and t-shirt she'd originally tried to put on, pointing out she probably wouldn't wear that to any kind of planned dinner, no matter who it was with. An impromptu dinner? Definitely. But there was no point in trying to rile her parents on purpose, just to make a point.

Todd had changed into a less formal button-down shirt made of a hunter green, soft jersey and a pair of khaki dress slacks, instead of the suit he'd originally planned on wearing. She'd changed into a button-down shirt and a soft flowing skirt that stopped well above her knees, which was probably part of the reason her mother's lips twitched.

"It's so lovely to see you, sweetheart," her mother said warmly, drawing her into a hug. The blandness of her words glossed over the fact it had literally been months since they'd seen each other. Allison's smile was a little frozen, especially when she saw her father coming down the hall from over her mother's shoulder.

He looked older than when she'd last seen him, somehow, more worn. The circles under his eyes seemed darker, and it looked like he had a few more wrinkles. Of course, he didn't have makeup or other alternatives like her mother to help him cover the tracks of age. Even knowing the signs of stress and age came from the amount of time he spent working and not from her absence, her heart twinged a little at the sight of him. Surely, her absence hadn't *helped*, although she didn't regret taking her leave rather than making her father's life less stressful by doing everything he wished.

"Allison," he said as her mother released her from their embrace.

"Father." Her mouth dry, she stood there for an awkward moment, unsure what to do. Then, a little stiffly, he held out his arms, and she stepped into another hug, feeling his body relax a little once she was hugging him back. Behind her, she could hear Todd and her mother exchanging a greeting.

The initial awkwardness was eventually smoothed over with small talk and drinks before dinner, her mother blithely assuming control of the conversation and catching Allison up on all the gossip about the many acquaintances she'd had no reason to hear about for months. On the one hand, it was a little annoying, but on the other, there was something soothing about letting her mother chatter aimlessly, keeping the conversation light.

It wasn't until they moved into the dining room the conversation turned to more serious matters. Of course, her father started by asking how Todd was doing at work, and from the questions he asked, she could tell they'd already had a conversation about Todd's career when Todd had talked to him before. To her surprise, her father didn't seem to condescend or patronize Todd, although he was perfectly willing to offer his advice. It seemed Todd had made more of an impression on her father than she'd realized.

"And how is your job?" her father asked, turning his attention to her. She gave a little start of surprise, not so much at his wanting to involve her in the conversation as the subject matter. In the past, her father had been more supportive of her working than her mother, but he hadn't shown any real interest to hear about it. "Do you think you'll stay where you are after graduation?"

"I'm not sure," she said slowly, trying to get her head around the fact she was now talking about her career with her father. Her mother looked on attentively rather than trying to change the subject or gently scolding Allison. Maybe they really had changed their views on her in the months she'd been gone. "For a little while, probably. I like what I do, but I don't think they need me full time and don't think I want a career in Human Resources, even though I enjoy it. I've been thinking about sending in some applications to publishing houses to see if I can get an entry-level position in one of those."

"Are you going to do that before or after graduation?" he asked.

"I was thinking I'd start before I graduate. I've already started looking at websites to see if they're hiring and keeping an eye on the major job sites to see if they advertise any openings. I'm sure there are other people who will also be sending in their resumes before graduation, but there's a lot of people who procrastinate. I'd rather be in the earlier group."

Her father nodded approvingly. Allison was taken aback at the expression of pride on his face; he was almost glowing. What on earth had changed while she was away? Before, he'd been supportive but not like this. Not only was he much friendlier and more open with Todd than she'd ever expected, but the approval fairly emanating from him wasn't what she was used to when it came to talking about jobs.

"Would you like me to look at your resume?"

It wasn't just her father. Her mother was beaming at both him and Allison, as if they were having a very clever conversation. Was it the fact Allison was engaged, and her mother was happy with whatever else she chose to do, or had Patrice truly missed her daughter so much, she didn't care what Allison did anymore?

"Yes… I would appreciate that," she said, trying to cover her surprise.

"Oh, surely, you can do more than that, dear," her mother said, reaching out to touch her father's hand. "Aren't you friends with—"

"No, it's okay, that's perfect," Allison interrupted. "I really appreciate it." She smiled at her mother to take any sting out of her words.

Although it would definitely make her life easier to use a little nepotism, that's not how she wanted to get her job. Right now, she felt like she had a bit of a leg up on most people in school, working part-time and getting experience to go along with her degree. If she really couldn't find something she wanted, maybe she'd allow her parents to help her with their connections. After all, a big part of the business world *was* connections, but she really wanted to try to do it on her own. More than anything, Allison was touched her parents wanted to help.

Her mother made a little face of disappointment but subsided without a fight, then brightened again. "Can we talk about the wedding now?"

Allison giggled at the pained look on her father's face. Listening to party planning wasn't his favorite thing, and she couldn't imagine a wedding would be any different. Todd smiled encouragingly, reaching out to cover Allison's hand with his own. She smiled back, giddy.

"When are you thinking?" her mother asked, her eyes glowing with approval as she looked from Todd to Allison.

"Ah..." Allison shot a glance at Todd. "We hadn't really talked about that yet." They'd been too busy having mad passionate sex, fighting, then having more mad passionate sex. While the fighting hadn't been pleasant, she could say she preferred the mad passionate sex to sitting down and trying to think about wedding planning particulars.

"Well, spring is always nice, but very busy... That would give us a full year to plan, though, which is just barely enough time."

"A year is barely enough time?" Todd looked amazed. Allison wasn't surprised, but then again, she was a girl. She'd watched enough wedding shows to know a lot more went into planning a wedding than most men realized. Okay... and researched it a little herself, although she was no longer particularly interested in having the giant wedding, she'd planned in her head when she'd done things like look through bridal magazines at dresses and venues.

"Oh, my, yes. Places book up a year in advance, sometimes more! Especially the best venues," her mother chirped, her eyes brightening as she warmed to her topic. "Allison will need to pick out her dress at least six months in advance, although more would be better, so there will be plenty of time to have it made, then altered if needed. We'll need to do a tasting for the food from at least three caterers for comparison, and the same for the cakes, then the flowers, the invitations, the officiant... Do you know if you want to be married in a church or somewhere else? By a member of the clergy or a judge? Oh, and you'll need to pick out a wedding party and tuxes and bridesmaid dresses, but before that, you'll have to decide on your colors. Oh, we can't forget we need to pick out favors. Something unique but not tacky. Announcements... we'll have to send out an engagement announcement and write up some-thing for the wedding announcement for the paper..."

The expression on Todd's face started to match Allison's fathers as her mother chattered on, and it was all Allison could do not to laugh. Her mother was babbling on so quickly, no one would have been able to get a word in edgewise if they'd wanted to, but at least Allison knew there wasn't a chance in hell she'd forget anything important during the planning process—not with Patrice Bradford as her mother.

"Oh, and dear," her mother put her hand over Todd's, beaming at him with all the happiness of a future mother-in-law hellbent on planning a wedding. "I'll need your mother's phone number."

"Um… of course."

Stifling her giggles, Allison decided she'd better step in and save the menfolk. Her father looked more and more pained the more her mother spoke, obviously finding it all too easy to envision the upcoming months of event planning.

Besides, Allison knew they needed to change topics if they were ever going to move on to dessert. Her mother seemed to have forgotten the purpose of dinner was eating.

"We'll have to talk about the rest of it and get back to you," she said smoothly as her mother paused for breath between explaining all the myriad of details that would need to be considered. "I think we'll focus on the big things first—date, budget, and guest list, then move on from there."

"Budget first," her mother trilled. Allison was a little surprised she wasn't bouncing in her seat, she was so happy. Obviously, she'd considered containing herself during the first part of dinner to be a duty well completed and was perfectly happy to commandeer the conversation, now that the end of dinner was approaching. "That will determine the venue and the number of people on the guest list. I can already tell you, I've put aside an account, and you have at least $60,000 to spend, although I'm sure your father and I wouldn't have a problem if you needed more."

Allison couldn't help but notice her mother completely ignored the way her husband's jaw clenched. Todd's jaw dropped, and Allison shook her head.

"That's way too much, Mom. I don't want or need a wedding that big."

Her mother waved a negligent hand as Todd blinked, still looking adorably stunned at the idea a wedding might actually cost that much. Allison knew all too well, weddings could cost even more, although she'd seen weddings just as wonderful without going to all that expense. At a certain point, no one cared if you spent two-hundred or two-thousand dollars on your flowers. Either way, the flowers were beautiful.

"Well, it's there for you to use. I thought you should know. And you might be grateful for it when you see our side of the guest list."

"Todd and I will talk about it," Allison said firmly. "But I want a *small* wedding, and by small, I don't mean less than three-hundred, I mean less than one-hundred-and-fifty people." Now Todd looked slightly horrified at the idea a small wedding could be up to one-hundred-fifty people, and Allison was having the hardest time not laughing. Her father's attention had obviously wandered. He had a blank look on his face that said he was thinking about anything other than the conversation at hand. Well, she really couldn't blame him.

"But how will we invite all of my friends and your father's business associates?" Her mother blinked, looking disappointed and confused.

"We won't."

"But—"

"Can we not talk about this now, please?" Allison pleaded a little. "Todd and I haven't even discussed a date, much less anything more detailed."

"Well... well, yes, of course," her mother said, obviously regrouping. The little furrow that appeared in her brow indicated she wasn't done arguing.

Allison wanted to talk with Todd, so they could get on the same page before her mother ended up taking over the entire planning process. Although she was sure her mother would plan a lovely wedding, it would end up going far beyond the original budget she'd indicated. The guest list would be enormous, with most people neither she nor Todd knew. Which, at one point in her life, Allison had assumed would be the wedding she would have. Now, it sounded overdone and unnecessary, not to mention, she'd rather have people she cared about than literally hundreds of people she would barely recognize.

"So, what about the honeymoon?" her mother asked, and Allison tried not to groan.

By the time Allison and Todd returned home, she felt a bit like a wrung-out rag, but happy. For the first time in a long time, there wasn't any negativity hovering over her head, nothing that made her feel angry or sad. Although neither she nor her parents had actually apologized during the evening, it was pretty clear both sides were ready to silently compromise and move on. Part of her still wished they'd apologized, but she could live without it. And it had been really nice to see them again.

"Thank you," she said, throwing her arms around Todd's waist as they walked up to their house. "I'm really glad we went."

"Good," he replied as he unlocked the door and pulled her inside. "Your mother is terrifying."

"You didn't notice that before?"

"I mostly talked to your dad when I went over there to talk about proposing to you. Your mother just dabbed at her eyes with a tissue. I thought the crying was frightening but good God, when she went into planning mode...."

"Ah," Allison said, smiling as she went up on her tiptoes to kiss him. "You'll get used to her."

"Apparently, I don't have much choice," he teased, shaking his head. Standing in the entryway to the house, he put his arms around her, looking down at her with an incredibly soft expression in his eyes. She tilted her head back for the kiss she was sure was coming. "So, when do you want to get married?"

She burst out laughing. "We don't *have* to decide on everything she talked about right now."

"But what if she calls tomorrow?"

"Oh, my goodness." Allison rolled her eyes. "You're actually terrified of my mom. I always thought my dad was scarier."

"He and I understand each other," Todd muttered as he pulled away and moved into the house, pulling her behind him. "Come on, let's go watch something mind-numbing, then you can explain to me what the hell she meant about wedding *colors*."

While Allison was picking out a movie, Todd listened to a voice-mail his mother had left while they'd been at dinner with her parents. Although his mother had known he was going to propose, he hadn't actually had a chance to talk to her during the day because of everything that had happened. And, of course, he'd had his phone turned off while they were having dinner with Allison's parents; anything else would have been impolite.

Groaning, he collapsed onto the couch, looking absolutely harried. Holding a DVD case in her hand, Allison arched an inquisitive eyebrow at him.

"She asked *every single question* your mom did," he said testily. "When, where, how many guests... what *colors*? What is it with you women and wedding colors?"

The poor man looked absolutely daunted. Allison launched herself onto his lap, giggling even harder as she wound her body around him. Apparently, the poor thing hadn't realized what a tizzy a wedding could send mothers into.

"Don't worry sweetheart, I'll protect you."

"You'd better," he growled. "Or I'll tan your bottom."

"Hey, you asked for it. Literally."

He rolled his eyes, then grunted as she poked him.

"Like, literally, you asked me to marry you."

Their eyes met, shining with the same teasing love, and Allison felt as though she could melt into a puddle of blissful joy.

"Yes, yes, I did."

10

Mr. & Mrs. Robert D. Bradford
request the honor of your presence
at the marriage of their daughter
Allison Elizabeth
to
Theodore Paul Rinald
Saturday, the twenty-sixth of January
at 5 o'clock in the evening
Reception to follow

Wedding—the art of compromise. At least that's how Allison had come to think of it.

Her parents were excited and proud at her graduation. They threw her a wonderful graduation party at their house, inviting a lot of people Allison didn't know, other than from her father's work-related parties, but that was okay because they all brought envelopes with checks. She and Todd had decided to use each and every one for Todd's further education.

After their wedding, he was going to go back to school for his masters. It was obvious the wedding was of bigger import to her mother. She spent the entire graduation party talking about it, even though Allison kept asking her not to. It seemed rude when she knew they wouldn't be inviting the majority of the people at the party, at least not all the business wives her mother kept talking to. Her mother hadn't quite accepted that yet.

April through July was really the big 'wedding' season, so they didn't have too much trouble finding a venue available for a winter wedding, despite her mother's dire predictions. The guest list was the next big issue, although when Allison said she'd rather pay for her own wedding if that meant she could get what she wanted, her parents gave in. One-hundred-fifty people were invited, and one hundred thirty-two were coming, all friends and family. She had relented and invited a few people from her father's business, his bosses and his work team, but none of his business acquaintances. This was about her and Todd, not about showing off for her father's friends.

She let her mother upgrade the meal... and the chairs for the reception... and the linens... and talk her into an overpriced dress —which was absolutely gorgeous, even if it was far too much money to spend on a dress she would only wear one day. But it kept her mother happy. Plus, she really did like the upgrades, even if she didn't think they were necessary.

Todd's mother was so thrilled her son was getting married, she had no special requests. Allison adored Todd's mother. To keep things on an even footing, she and Todd decided to pay for their mother's dresses as a gift, and Allison's mother and Mrs. Rinald— Allison was still having trouble calling her Tess as she'd requested— bonded over dress shopping, without any of the snobbishness Allison had worried about from her side of the family. It seemed as though her parents really were changing, just a little.

The biggest drama actually came from Allison's friend, Chrissy, who was incensed Diana had been asked to be the Maid of Honor while she was "only" a bridesmaid, then tried to take over planning the bridal shower and bachelorette party. Poor Diana had her hands full dealing with her. Fortunately, as the bride, Allison was able to stay out of it. Not that Chrissy didn't try to recruit her support, but

Allison had no problem disappointing her, telling her should talk to Diana about. It got to the point, she started hoping Chrissy would throw enough of a fit, she would resign her position as a bridesmaid. The other two bridesmaids weren't too impressed with Chrissy, either, and eventually, Chrissy figured out she needed to calm the eff down and try to play nice.

By the day of the wedding, everyone was smiling and getting along famously—or at least faking it enough for Allison's purposes. It was her own fault for asking Chrissy to be a bridesmaid. She'd known what Chrissy was like before she'd made the decision to include her in the bridal party. Expecting Chrissy to be anything other than herself was ludicrous. Deep down, their friendship was strong enough, Chrissy stopped playing the spoiled brat and put on her best face for her friend.

Yesterday, they'd gone to the nail salon en masse for mani-pedis. Chrissy had tried to persuade all of them to get the same color, but Allison had said she couldn't care less, and they'd ended up choosing whatever color they wanted. She was starting to suspect when Chrissy got married, she really did *not* want to be a bridesmaid. It was all too easy to picture her bridesmaidzilla as a bridezilla.

Today was hair, followed by makeup, then pictures. Hair was another thing Allison had let her bridesmaids choose for themselves. Her own was done up in a loose curly style, pinned to the back of her head with tendrils trailing down in the very back and along the sides. Somehow, the entire thing stayed secure when she moved, despite all those hanging tendrils. It was a very soft style with one loose curl on each side to frame her face, very romantic looking, especially with her dress.

She'd managed to find one with straps. Strapless always made her worry she was going to spend all night tugging on it. The dress was basically backless, the straps wrapping around her shoulders and connecting to the front of the dress under her arms. A demure sweetheart neckline made the front appear much more innocent than the back. The skirt was a full A-line—made fuller by the crino-line underneath—and had a detachable chapel-length train. Little pearl beads and embroidery decorated the dress—along the waistline, on the straps, and little pockets of it around the skirt. It was a wonderful combination of traditional in the front and sexy in the back.

Since the back was so dramatic, she'd decided to wear a bird-cage veil, pinned in place with a pearl-encrusted comb. All the girls oohed and aahed once the veil was in place, and she got teary when she looked in the mirror. She looked every inch a *bride*. Even the hair and makeup trial hadn't given her this glowing, glorious image.

As excited as she'd been about getting married, Allison was really starting to wish they could just get the day over with. She was a bride, and she wanted to see her groom damnit. Other than the rehearsal dinner last night, she hadn't seen Todd in almost forty-eight hours and didn't count the rehearsal dinner as quality time. They'd had fun, but they'd always been surrounded by their family and the wedding party—not exactly conducive to quality time together. The whole 'not seeing the groom before the wedding' was getting real old… real fast.

Still, she tried to quell her impatience as the photographer arrived and took pictures of her, followed by pictures of her and her bridesmaids, then her and her parents. Her father looked quite impressive in his tux, his eyes already looking suspiciously pink. The dark purple dress her mother wore made her look younger than she was, and she glowed with happiness almost as much as Allison. The bridesmaids were each in the dresses they picked out. Allison had chosen a dark red, then allowed them the run of the store, as long as they picked a floor-length dress in that color. They'd ended up in different styles that suited each of them. Diana was wearing a silver satin sash, the 'accent' color for the wedding and a way to mark her out as the Maid of Honor.

Allison's bouquet was a stunning array of white lilies and red roses, studded with small gems that made it seem as though it was glittering. The bridesmaids carried white roses, also studded with gems.

After the pictures, the women were relegated to the bridal dressing room while the men arrived to get their pictures done. They'd wanted to get as many pictures as possible before the ceremony without Todd and her seeing each other, so they wouldn't keep the guests waiting too long between the ceremony and reception. Of course, they were having a cocktail hour, but they really didn't want that to go longer than an hour at the most.

Once the pictures were over, there wasn't much to do but sit around and wait for the ceremony. It was agony, knowing Todd was somewhere in the building, having his picture taken and not being able to see him. Fortunately, Tess had brought snacks while they were waiting, figuring they might be hungry. Gathering around the table to talk and gossip helped the time to pass a little faster.

When it was time to go downstairs, Tess gave her a kiss on the cheek, then flitted off to go see her son. Allison's mother hugged her tightly before heading down with her father—he said was going to wait for Allison down there. She was pretty sure he just wanted to make sure her mother was going to be okay—she seemed constantly on the verge of tears today—happy tears, but still. Allison's heart pounded as the rest of the bridesmaids headed downstairs, each giving her a hug on the way, then she and Diana were left alone.

"I can't believe it's finally here," said Diana.

Allison laughed. "You're telling me! This has been the longest day ever."

"Well, that too," Diana said, giggling. "You've been the very epitome of patience, though."

"Only because I don't have another choice," Allison said with a heartfelt groan. "May I recommend an early morning wedding?"

The wedding coordinator poked her head into the room. "We're ready for you now, ladies. He's at the altar."

"So much trouble, just to make sure I can't see my groom," Allison muttered as she moved toward the door.

"You were the one to insist on that," Diana reminded her.

"It seemed like a good idea at the time."

As much as Allison had changed, she found she was a pretty traditional person during the wedding planning process. Fortunately, so was Todd. They had opted not to do a "First Look," as tempting as it was. They liked the idea of her walking down the aisle and seeing each other for the first time. For the same reason, they hadn't spent last night together. Allison had spent it at her parents' house with Diana to help keep her distracted. The idea of waking up in bed with Todd on the wedding day just seemed somehow wrong. While she was sure plenty of other people enjoyed it, she wanted today to be different from other days. Waking up without Todd next to her was definitely different.

She just hadn't realized how frustrating it would be.

They arrived outside the hall where Allison's father was waiting, the last bridesmaid and groomsman, her friend, Mary, from work and her step-cousin, Chad, walking through the door. Diana gave her a squeeze and then got into position, stepping forward when the wedding coordinator gave her the nod. As soon as Diana had stepped through, the coordinator closed the doors, so Allison and her father could get into position. He looked dashing in his tux, and she was glad her mother had insisted he wear one rather than a black suit, which he thought he would have preferred.

She curled her hand over her father's elbow, her heart pounding as she stared at the doors in front of her.

"I'm very proud of you," her father said, barely loud enough for her to hear. "I don't think I say that often enough."

Blinking through the tears forming in her eyes, Allison looked up at him, feeling as if she might actually fall apart.

"Thank you, Daddy."

"I love you."

"I love you, too."

"Are you ready?"

Emotion surged, and her throat closed up. She couldn't find the words to speak, so she just nodded. They both looked at the wedding coordinator, who gave Allison an encouraging smile and knocked lightly on the door, and her helpers swung them open.

The room was filled with people, who all turned and stood, blocking most of her view, but at the very end of the aisle, she could see him. Her vision seemed to surge, and she took in a deep breath, knowing this next step was going to be the first one into the next part of her life. The white runner shone against the dark red of the carpet, clearer than any yellow brick road. As her father tugged her forward, she was barely aware of anything but the man standing ahead of her, waiting for her to come to him and pledge to be his forever.

~

"Well, Mrs. Allison Rinald? What do you think?" Todd asked as he maneuvered her around the dance floor. The lessons her mother had insisted on had been a complete waste, Allison decided. Todd was moving great, but even wearing a long skirt to the lessons hadn't prepared Allison to dance in a *wedding* dress. Between the layers and the hint of train, even bustling her dress couldn't completely get rid of, she wasn't moving at all like she was supposed to.

"I think we should have had a morning wedding."

Laughing, Todd twirled her around, and she did her best not to trip. One good thing about her wedding dress, people probably weren't aware she was missing her steps because there was no way they could see her feet. As long as she didn't trip, no one would know anything was amiss—hopefully.

"I missed you too, Princess," he said as he pulled her in tightly, the cheers and catcalls from around the dance floor melding into general noise. Despite the fact they were the center of attention, it was the most private moment they'd had in three days, and Allison was relishing it. It was a good thing she did. After their first dance together, they didn't have another private moment for the rest of the reception.

It had taken the wedding coordinator's professional acumen to get them to the first area where they'd be taking pictures. One could argue, they had time for a few private words while the photographer was taking pictures of just the two of them, but they also had a photographer and an audience. The entire situation had been absurd, sending them into random fits of giggles, which made for some wonderful wedding photos. The wedding coordinator hustled them into place to enter the reception.

The first dance was followed by much-needed sustenance,

speeches between the salad and entrée courses, which they had to scarf down, so they could walk around and greet their guests. They finally made it back to the dance floor, but it was very crowded, and everyone wanted a turn dancing with the bride and groom. Even when they did manage to come together, they were surrounded by people watching them—this time, from a few inches away rather than the edge of the dance floor, but that didn't dim Allison's happiness.

Blissful energy seemed to overflow from her and Todd, leaking out across the room, infecting everyone. There wasn't a single person who didn't have a smile on their face, and to Allison's shock, her mother and father joined the crowded dance floor, even after the music changed from big band to more current offerings. Her dad obviously had no idea how to dance to modern music, but he seemed to enjoy trying, and she was even happier, she'd insisted on the wedding being only friends and family. She didn't think he would have cracked his usual stodgy veneer if any important acquaintances had been invited. His boss was also on the dance floor, which seemed to give free rein to the few employees invited.

Grinning, Allison turned back to Todd, tipping her head back for a kiss. They couldn't truly indulge, in the middle of the dance floor, but it was better than nothing.

After leaving the ceremony, Allison was so overcome with happiness, she'd accidentally left Diana standing there, holding her bouquet rather than taking it back from her. She and Todd had only had time for one private moment of staring into each other's eyes before their bridal party joined them, followed swiftly by the rest of their guests, and of course, everyone wanted to say congratulations.

EPILOGUE

*T*odd pressed her against the wall, the moment they got into their hotel room.

"Finally," he said, letting out his breath as he pressed his lips against hers. They'd ended up running by the time they reached the hallway to their room, giggling madly like little kids as they escaped the mass of people who had wanted to give them one last hug or word of congratulations. How was it possible, people didn't realize newlyweds would want to escape to their wedding night? Every second of waiting had seemed like an eternity.

His lips devoured hers, a needy intensity more intimate and meaningful than any other kiss they'd shared. His hands were tight on her hips, drawing her against him, her thighs parted just enough to cradle him in her softness. Allison steadied herself on his shoulders, moaning as his lips left hers and moved down the sensitive skin of her neck, salty and sweet from dancing. With half-hooded eyes, her head turned, and her eyes widened.

"Todd, look!"

She broke away from his embrace, ignoring his dismayed groan, and darted into the room. At some point during the evening, she'd noticed Diana had disappeared, but she hadn't realized her friend had come here. At least she assumed this was Diana, although she wouldn't be surprised if others had been involved.

The honeymoon suite was in two parts. They were in the main room, and in the back left corner was the entrance to the bedroom. The main room had a couch along the right wall, a loveseat at a right angle to the couch, facing her, with a coffee table set in front of them, across from which was a table with a large television. The coffee table had been decorated with electronic candles, which were flickered just like real ones, a silver bucket with champagne, two glasses, and a small plate of chocolate-covered strawberries. There was also a vase holding a single red rose in the center.

"Ooooh, it's so romantic!" she gushed, stopping just shy of the coffee table and looking it over. Tears sparked in her eyes again. Normally, she wasn't this emotional, but everything was setting her off today. It was a wonder she hadn't sobbed through the ceremony, although she'd sniffled enough, Diana had surreptitiously passed her a tissue sometime in the middle of it.

"Yes, it is," Todd said as he wrapped his arms around her from behind, his lips going to her neck and sucking, using his teeth to good effect. He obviously had his own agenda, and it didn't include anything on the coffee table.

"Todd," she half-protested, moaning. Her hands covered his wrists as he pulled her flush against him. Despite the layers of her A-line skirt and crinoline, she could still feel his erection pressing into her ass. "We should drink the champagne... have a strawberry... Someone went to all the trouble to set this up..." She wasn't really resisting, she just liked the idea of him convincing her of his way of thinking—taking control of the situation—and she had no doubt he would do just that.

"You have no idea how hard it has been to keep my hands off of you all night," he murmured, pulling her around and holding her hips tightly as he kissed over her collarbone. Her hands rested on his shoulders, and she wasn't sure if she was pulling him into her or pushing him away. "Seeing you in this white dress, looking so pure and innocent... all I could think about were all the depraved, perverted things I wanted to do to you while you were wearing it."

Allison gasped as he pushed down the neckline of her dress, folding it almost inside out. The heart-shaped neckline was helpful, although her strap pulled on her shoulder as he basically lifted her breast out of the dress. She wasn't wearing a bra because the dress had one built-in, and right now, she was even more thankful for that. Expertly, Todd did the same with her other breast as his mouth pulled at her nipple, his other hand splayed over her lower back, holding her in place as she arched backward, thrusting her breast farther into his mouth.

"Are you sure you don't want me to take it off?" she asked, panting as he switched his attention to her other breast, lavishing both of her nipples with all of his pent-up sexual energy. The champagne and strawberries could wait. Todd's sensual need was too intoxicating to deny. Feasting on her breasts like a starving man, her knees were feeling weaker by the second.

"Definitely not," he growled, hooking his arm around her waist and pulling her over to the side of the loveseat, where he whirled her around and bent her over the wide arm. Allison made a little "oof" as she found her upper body dropping down unexpectedly, her hard nipples rubbing against the nubby fabric of the cushion, her breasts high and tight from being pushed out of her dress. Cool air wrapped around her legs as he lifted her skirts. "I've been waiting to do this all night."

"I could at least take off the crinoline," she said, trying to wriggle her way up, but Todd just tipped the skirts over her head and pushed her back down, creating a dark little cave she was caught in. He let out a laugh, and she grinned, knowing he must be seeing her special panties. White with a little ruffle on each leg opening and "Bride" across the butt in silver.

"No, I don't want you to take anything off," he said, running his fingers up the backs of her thighs and making her shiver. "I want you just like this... all dressed up in your pretty white dress, ready for me to take and corrupt you."

The dark eroticism in his voice, the eagerness, brought Allison back to the beginning of their encounters, when Todd had 'blackmailed' her into fulfilling her most secret fantasies. He'd taken the sweet little society girl she'd been and let her loose, pushing her beyond the lines she'd always lived in, and bringing her to wild pleasures beyond her imagination.

Now, she could imagine how she looked, bent over the armrest of a loveseat, unseen except for her legs and turned up butt cheeks, a fantasy of visual innocence about to be debauched. Just imagining it made her feel hot all over.

She moaned as Todd pulled down her panties, his mouth following them down, tracing patterns on her skin with his tongue and lingering on her most sensitive spots—the crease between her buttocks and thigh, the ticklish inner edge behind her knees, then back up again to tease her pouting lips. With a whimper, she spread her legs wider, inviting him to taste, and trembled with satisfaction as his tongue delved in. Hands kneaded her thighs, pushing them farther apart, then moved up to her bottom, squeezing her tender cheeks hard. As he built her pleasure with his mouth, his fingers became rougher, adding an edge to their passion.

When he pulled away, she whimpered and wagged her hips, her fingers clutching the skirts of her dress around her head, hating that she couldn't see him, yet loving the visual in her mind and enjoying the blindness, the anticipation.

Something cool and slick pressed against her asshole, and she moaned as his fingers pushed in, stretching and lubricating her heated flesh.

"Where did you get lube from?" she asked, her voice only muffled by the layers of fabric. She had the wild image of him pledging his wedding vows with lube in his suit pocket.

Todd just chuckled, twisting his fingers and making her whimper. "It's our wedding night, Princess. You don't think I'd be prepared for anything?"

The first time they'd had sex, he'd taken her anal virginity. There was something so decadently forbidden, so depraved about taking his cock in her ass, she wasn't surprised he wanted to defile her innocent appearance. Even having his fingers penetrating her there while she bent over the loveseat in her virginal white dress was shockingly exciting. It added an edge she hadn't felt since the first few times he'd taken her that way.

He only took a minute or two to stretch her before his fingers pulled away. Allison moaned at the loss, her butt cheeks clenching and releasing enticingly. The hot, hard head of his cock prodded her entrance, then pressed in, pushing her much farther open than his fingers had. She groaned at the intrusion and panted, trying to relax her muscles to accommodate his thick girth. Practice had helped, and after a moment, his broad head popped through the ring of muscle, both of them moaning with the sensation. Todd's fingers dug into her hips as he pressed forward, the burning shaft digging deeper into her most intimate of entrances.

Knowing he couldn't see more than the curve of her bottom, bisected by his cock as it pillaged her tight hole, and the layers of crinoline skirts, made Allison even more excited. She drew her hands down to pinch her nipples, pulling and tugging on the tender buds, gasping and writhing as Todd's cock quested deeper. The thick shaft radiated heat as it continued its burning exploration, rubbing against her insides as he made small thrusting motions, helping to stretch her further.

"God, Allison... you have no idea how hot this is." His voice ragged with passion, he pulled out, then thrust back in hard, his groin slamming against her ass cheeks and making them wobble. "Aw... fuck... I'm fucking my wife in the ass... God, you're so tight..." He pulled out again and groaned, thrusting back in hard.

His wife. The words sent a tremor through her like none she'd ever known, heating her insides to the point, she thought she might cum. Pinching her nipples hard, Allison let out a gasping cry as he began to ride her, assured she could take the stretching, burning thrusts of his cock in her narrow passage without undue pain. It hurt, it hurt exquisitely, wonderfully. He was claiming her with every thrust, his muttered words barely audible, but she could hear *wife* over and over again. She pinched her nipples harshly, her excited cries mingling with his words.

"Oh, fuck..." She writhed, her pussy feeling like it might actually explode with need. It burned from the assault on her other hole, emptily grasping... needing... yet her orgasm built. Todd's cock nudging against a point deep inside of her spurred her pleasure higher and higher.

"Todd... oh, fuck... fuck me... fuck your wife... fuck my ass! AH!" Her back bowed as he lost all control of his thrusts, beginning a wild, ramming assault on her tender hole and sending her spiraling with a hot ecstasy that bloomed from her forbidden orifice and had her muscles clamping down hard. The animalistic noises falling from his throat were almost lost in her delicious cries.

She shattered around him as he embedded himself fully, her body sucking at him as he poured hot froth into her welcoming hole. His fingers were grasping her so hard, she would have light bruises the next morning, but all they could feel right now was pure ecstasy, an intimate bliss that left no room for anything but rapture —a meeting of desires, passions, and souls that had been acknowledged privately and publicly.

To her surprise, Todd didn't collapse on top of her as he normally did. Instead, he rubbed her hips soothingly as their breathing returned to normal and pulled free of her body. He pulled down her skirts and unzipped the back of her dress, his movements hurried as if he couldn't bear having even those layers of fabric between them.

Allison allowed him to pull her up as the dress fell around her, leaving her standing in the pooled fabric as Todd's lips descended. They kissed deeply, passionately, but no longer quite so demandingly. The hurried need of several days abstinence and the excitement of publicly acknowledging their commitment was no longer there. Sated, they could take the time to taste each other, enjoy each other.

His hands cradling her face, Todd caressed her lips with his, his fingers slowly stroking over her cheeks and jawbone as they explored each other's mouths all over again. This wasn't new territory, but somehow, it felt like it. Allison ruffled her fingers through the hair on his chest. They touched each other lightly, not teasingly but lovingly, as if they had all the time in the world—which now, they did.

"Come on," Todd murmured finally. "Let's take a shower, then we can have strawberries and champagne."

Sighing, Allison shot a wistful glance at the arrangement on the coffee table, then followed him willingly.

The shower revived them, allowing them to rediscover each other's bodies as they washed, cleaning every inch of the other. It was a relief for Allison to wash out her hair, which had a massive amount of hairspray. She hadn't realized how much the updo was bothering her head until Todd's strong fingers massaged her scalp. Neither of them realized quite how tired they were until they were wrapped in towels and seated on the couch, feeding each other strawberries through their yawns.

"No, stop it!" Todd batted at her as she tried to shove some of the fruit into his gaping mouth, laughing madly. Being tired had made her more than a little punchy, and she was having far too much fun, trying to annoy him. "I was yawning, not asking for more!"

"Are you sure?" she teased. "That's not what it looked like."

"You, Princess, are going the right way for a spanking, and that's not how I wanted to end the night."

She pouted at him. "Why not?"

"Because it didn't seem right to spank you on our wedding night."

"Oh, but you'll fuck me in the ass?" She laughed and tried to shove another strawberry in his mouth, amused by his indignant expression.

"Well, I wasn't planning on *that*, either, if you must know... but then I flipped up your skirts, and you have such a pretty little asshole... It seemed like the most depraved thing I could do to you at the moment." He grinned broadly, smugly, looking remarkably like a certain fictional cat—one that had just eaten an entire bowl of cream.

"And I quite enjoyed it," Allison purred, giving him her most seductive look, which was quite ruined when she yawned widely. True to form, Todd retaliated with his own strawberry as she tried to cover her mouth.

"I think it's time for bed, Princess," he said firmly.

"I want to spend more time with you! I don't want to go to sleep yet. This was seriously the longest day ever, and I feel like I didn't get to spend nearly enough of it with you." Allison pouted, knowing he was going to insist. And really, she shouldn't be arguing. She knew she was acting a little childish, but it came so naturally when she was completely exhausted.

"Me, too," he said as he scooped her up from the couch, not giving her an option about whether she was going to be headed for the bedroom. "But we have plenty of time to spend together over the next two weeks—just us, no friends or family."

Allison smiled as she nestled her head against his shoulder, her hair only half dry. They were going on a Mediterranean cruise, halfway around the world from all the people who could take his attention away from her. He was finally going to show her Turkey. Not only that, but only one of the stops was somewhere he'd been before, so they would see everything else for the first time together. She couldn't wait.

Of course, all of those thoughts were driven from her mind when Todd peeled the towel away from her and laid her down on the bed, covering her almost immediately with his body. Despite the fact she was tired, she responded to the lovely feel of his weight, his skin pressing against her. The wiry hairs on his chest tickled her nipples and breasts as he kissed her insistently. She kissed him back happily, a bit more awake than she was thirty seconds before.

Parting her legs, she felt him nudging against her, already hard and eager to be buried inside her. With a low moan, she tilted her hips, but he didn't take the obvious invitation.

"We don't *have* to do this tonight, you know," she teased. "If you're too tired.

"It's our wedding night, and we are consummating this marriage," he said in a no-nonsense voice.

"Well, you might have thought of that when you had me bent over the couch."

"I did and decided I should consummate our marriage there as well."

She laughed, but then his mouth was on hers again, and she gave way to the breathless kissing, feeling his weight and hips shift as he found her center and began to push in. Her legs spread wider to welcome him home, because that's what they had become for each other.

As they crossed the finish line together, moaning and panting, Allison knew that she'd finally found her happy ending.

~

I hope you enjoyed Allison and Todd's story!
If you want more naughty coeds, make sure to CLICK here to check out my boxset of them!

ABOUT THE AUTHOR

Sinister Ange is a *USA Today* best-selling author and the alternate pen name for Golden Angel. She is happily married, old enough to know better but still too young to care, and a big fan of happily-ever-afters, strong heroes and heroines, and sizzling chemistry.

She believes the world is a better place when there's a little magic in it.

www.sinistreange.com

SINISTRE ANGE'S BOOKS

Sinistre Ange Books
      Standalone Stories
Alien Pleasures
Annie and the Sybian
Consequences - Part 1
Consequences - Part 2
Naughty Coeds Boxset
Dark Tales Boxset
Dominated by the Bull
His Omega Babygirl

Black Light
      Black Light: Roulette Rematch

Planets Apart
      His Favorite Hucow: Hathor
Amaya's Old-Fashioned Daddy: Hebe

His Pretty Kitty: Seirios
Taking the Reins: Xanthos

H appily Never After with Raisa Greywood
        Demon Lust
Blood Lust

Made in United States
Troutdale, OR
07/25/2023

11541774R00087